Cherish St. Maarten

A Cherish Cruises Sweet Romance

Cherish St. Maarten

LYNETTE PAUL

STORY VEIN

STORYVEIN

Published 2020 by StoryVein LLC

www.StoryVein.com

ISBN 978-1-951758-02-8

For all my siblings

CONTENTS

~ 1 ~

KNOCKIN' ON HEARTBREAK'S DOOR

I KNOCKED EXCITEDLY on Shayne's apartment door. He lived two buildings over in my apartment complex. Unlike me, he didn't have a roommate, so we spent more time hanging out at his place than mine, and tonight we had a very specific agenda—packing. Tomorrow we would leave Austin behind for a week-long Christmas cruise with my family. This was the first time I was bringing a boyfriend to Christmas, and I could not wait for everyone to meet him. They were going to love him as much as I did. He was a fellow yoga instructor at the studio I taught at, and we had pretty much everything in common. He couldn't be more perfect for me.

"Kate. You're early," he said as he swung the door open. In prana pants and an oversized sweatshirt, he was my vision of Mr. Right—all comfort and confidence.

1

I held up the bag of takeout from our favorite Indian restaurant on the corner. "I thought we might as well have dinner while we get you packed."

"Always so thoughtful." He ran his hand through his spiky black hair. It still looked wet.

Maybe I hadn't given him enough time to relax after class. I should have called first. I knew better than anyone that sometimes you needed a breather after teaching, especially around the holidays when all the students were running through their to-do lists in their heads instead of focusing on breathing through the poses. "I thought you'd be hungry," I said as I stood awkwardly in the hallway.

"Oh, yeah, I am. Sorry." He backed up and let me into his apartment.

I went straight to his kitchen to pull out a couple of plates to serve up our dinner. I also leaned my carefully wrapped present for him against the kitchen island. I didn't want to risk spilling our food all over it. I had spent the weekend putting the finishing touches on a watercolor painting of him in his favorite yoga pose, Warrior II. It'd taken forever to get the contented bliss on his face and the contours of his muscular limbs just right, but he would love it, and he was totally worth the effort. I knew he'd want to hang it in the yoga nook in his apartment. I wanted it to bring him as much joy when he practiced as he brought to me every day.

"I hope you're in the mood for garlic naan because they gave me a double order. I also brought your present to open early. It's a little bulky to pack for the cruise."

"Um, great." Shayne settled in on a stool on the other side of the island while I dished out the rice and butter chicken, giving him twice as much as me. He always had a huge appetite after teaching, and he'd done a double shift this afternoon to cover for the studio owner who'd needed to go to her daughter's Christmas play.

I handed him a fork and sat the plate in front of him. "Are you ready to get packed? I managed to get everything of mine in a carry-on this afternoon, so we won't have any baggage fees. I'm sure we can do the same for you. It's the tropics. We don't need much."

He laid the fork down and stared at the chicken.

"Have you even started packing?" I asked as I popped a piece of naan in my mouth.

He sighed and slipped off the stool to come around to the other side of the counter and stand face to face with me. "I haven't."

He looked entirely too serious about that.

I swallowed the bite of bread and said as cheerfully as I could, "That's okay. That's what I'm here for. We'll find your sunscreen and flip flops and have you ready in no time."

"About that." He paused and refused to meet my eyes.

My heart leapt into my throat. I knew that look. I had seen it before. Every guy. Every single one that I'd ever dated got that look at some point. The it's-not-you-it's-me frown. "No. Shayne. Do not say it. Do not do this to me right now." Visions of spending the next week very alone with my very perfect family danced through my head.

He met my eyes then and took my hands in his. "Kate, I really like you. You know that. We've had a great time together the last few months, but I can't go on this vacation with you."

"Are you kidding me? It's the night before our flight. We're supposed to catch a boat in Miami tomorrow. What do you mean you can't go?"

"I've been trying to think of the right way to tell you this."

How long had he been thinking about this? Days? Weeks? How long had my perfect guy been plotting to break up with me the night before my family's Christmas vacation? That made him seem a lot less flawless in hindsight.

"I don't want to let you down," he said. "I know how important this trip with your family is. I know you want it to be the best ever."

I sighed deeply. Mostly I wanted to prove that I was not a lost cause in my parents' eyes when held up against my overachieving siblings. My brother and sister both had great careers and promising futures. My sister, the doctor, had married a surgeon over the summer and moved into her dream home in Dallas. My brother was primed to take over the sales division of one of the fastest growing online retailers on the planet. And I was a part-time yoga instructor with vague hopes of running my own studio someday. Bringing my very serious boyfriend, who I had thought might propose sometime in the near future—like maybe on this cruise—was the only thing I had going for me to even come close to measuring up to their life successes.

"So come," I said.

He shook his head. "I can't, Kate. It would be a lie, and we can't do that to each other. I respect you too much. There's someone else."

I dropped his hands and rubbed at my temples. Boyfriends who respect their girlfriends don't start dating other people behind their backs. "How can there be someone else? How is this happening?"

"I never meant for this to happen. Willow and I went out for coffee after class the other day. She had some great insight about my approach to instruction. You know she trained under Seane Maze for Dynamic Vinyasa. She and I truly connected, like at a spiritual level." When he said Willow's name, his eyes got that dreamy quality about them that every girl wishes a guy would have about her.

I wanted him to think about me that way. Not her.

"Willow? Seriously?" I asked. She was the newest instructor at the studio. She'd been there for a total of two weeks, and everyone was infatuated with her, including my boyfriend apparently.

"The guilt has been killing me. I fell for her the day she walked into the studio. I tried to dismiss it as a crush, but it's not. It's really love with her. There's no denying it."

"You love her?" *And not me.* That's what he was saying. Whatever this had been between us had not been the real thing. I had completely misread how he felt about me because I assumed it was the same way I felt about him.

"We're going to spend Christmas at her parents' meditation center outside of Boulder."

Of course they were, because that's where gorgeous young yoga instructors named Willow spent their holidays. I couldn't listen to any more of what he had to say. I didn't want to hear how he had fallen in love with her. I could hardly breathe. I could hardly see with the tears clouding my vision. I grabbed my purse and headed for the door, leaving behind the still warm takeout, the painting I'd poured my heart into, and the guy who had torn my heart out.

I ran down five flights of stairs and out into the drizzling Austin night. What had just happened? An hour ago, I was happily in a relationship, looking forward to Christmas with my family for once. Suddenly I was single and dreading the family vacation more than ever. I did not want to see the disappointment on Mom and Dad's faces when I showed up alone. Again.

They had been high school sweethearts, so I knew they were mystified by why I was pushing thirty without a hint of anyone to share my future with. I wished I knew.

I sucked in a deep breath and let the tears roll down my face with the splatters of rain as I moped back to my own building. I didn't know what to do with myself. I didn't want to spend the holidays alone with my overly perfect family and their condolences for my derailed love life, but it didn't seem like I had much of a say in that now.

By the time I got back to my apartment, I was a sopping mess and at a complete loss. So I did the only thing I could think to do. I called the one person I could always count on—my best friend, Josh.

~ 2 ~

DOUBLE FUDGE COOKIE FRAPPUCCINO TROUBLE

JOSH WALLIS HAD been my best friend since the first day of high school. We'd both been new at Crockett High, and he'd saved me from a truly embarrassing encounter with the mean girl clique that I had inadvertently tried to sit with at lunch. His uncanny ability to breeze through awkward social situations came from a lifetime of hopping from one school to the next as his dad got transferred from base to base by the Army. We'd made fast friends that day and stuck by each other's side through high school and off to college. At Baylor, he studied finance, and I studied every way to fail at a relationship, but officially my degree was in general liberal arts. That was academic code for I had no idea what to do with my life, but I had enough credits to graduate.

We ended up both settling back in Austin a few blocks from each other. He took his business degree and his love for caffeine and opened a hip coffee shop on South Congress, and I taught classes at a yoga studio downtown. Fifteen years from our first auspicious meeting, he was still the one I counted on the most.

When I called that night, he picked up on the first ring.

"Kate," he practically sang into the phone. "I didn't expect to hear from you till after your big Christmas vacation in the tropics. What's up?"

"Josh," I only got his name out before I burst into breathless tears. I laid the phone on my coffee table and buried my head in my hands.

"Are you okay? Where are you?" His suddenly worried voice sounded depressingly far away on speaker.

"Yes," I managed to get out as I plucked another tissue out of the box and sniffled into it. "I'm home."

"Okay, hold on."

He gave some muffled instructions to one of his baristas in the background, and I glanced at the clock on my phone. I'd called him in the middle of closing. I hadn't even thought about that. He didn't seem worried about it though when he came back on the phone.

"Tell me what's wrong. Is this mint chocolate latte trouble or double fudge cookie frappuccino trouble?"

"Both." I managed a small laugh through my tears. Then I launched into the whole breakup story. I gave him every last detail, down to the meticulously wrapped painting that was now leaning abandoned against Shayne's kitchen island.

"I am so sorry." Josh's words were full of heartfelt sympathy.

He understood how much I'd been looking forward to vacationing with Shayne and introducing him to my brother and sister on the cruise. All last Friday, while we were sorting donations for the neighborhood toy drive, he'd listened to me rave nonstop about it.

"I don't know what to do. I don't even want to face the family right now. I can't go on this vacation with them."

He sighed. "You know it will break your mom's heart if you cancel on her. She wants your whole family together for the holiday. It's all she talked about when I stopped by with the pies on Thanksgiving."

"I know. I know," I groaned. "What am I supposed to do?"

He paused. I could picture him standing behind the counter in his empty coffee shop, drumming his fingers on the reclaimed barnwood counter, thinking of a kind way to tell me what I didn't want to hear— that I had to go on this trip sans boyfriend.

"What time is your flight in the morning?" he asked.

"Uh." I ran my fingers through my damp hair and tried to remember what my itinerary was supposed to be. "It's at ten-ish. Why?"

"I'll pick you up at seven thirty."

I tried to protest. I did not want to ruin his holiday. That wasn't why I'd called. I just wanted a shoulder to cry on, but that wasn't Josh's style. He was an all-in kind of guy. On a moment's notice, he reorganized his entire Christmas week, packed a bag, and headed to Miami with me so I wouldn't be all awkwardly alone with my family on Christmas.

By two o'clock the next afternoon, we were standing in line at the Miami cruise port, waiting to check in for the cruise to St. Maarten. The embarkation building was enormous, but elegantly decorated with a classy undersea motif, and the cruise line had processing a couple thousand passengers at a time down to a science. We'd only been in line a few minutes and were nearly to the front. I kind of wished they were slower. Putting off meeting up with my family and their pitying looks for a while longer wouldn't be such a bad thing.

"I'm cursed," I said.

Josh rubbed my shoulder. "You aren't cursed. You just need to find the right guy."

I looked up into his puppy dog brown eyes and whined, "I thought I had the perfect guy."

He brushed my hair off my neck like he could brush away my disappointment. "There is no perfect guy, Kate. There's the right guy for you. And you'll find him."

I wished I shared his optimism. "How do you know? You haven't found the right girl."

Josh's love life had never been as erratic as mine. He tended to date less often and more seriously, but he hadn't had a special someone for a while. I didn't understand why. Josh had that everyman handsome quality about him. He was the lovable, attractive, boy-next-door type that would sweep some lucky girl off her feet someday.

"I've always got my eyes open." He glanced around hopefully. "Maybe she's on this cruise."

"That would be my luck. I bring you along for a shoulder to cry on, and you fall in love with a dance instructor or something."

Josh scratched at the scruff on his chin as though he were in deep thought about that. "I do like to dance."

I laughed. "And you, my friend, are horrible at it."

Then it was our turn to check in. A chipper Cherish Cruises staffer in a blue and pink uniform waved us over to her check-in station, and the whole process went surprisingly smoothly, considering Josh was a last-minute substitution. I thought there might be a fuss about that, but apparently he had talked to my mom last night, and they had already worked it out with the cruise line.

"Thanks for calling her," I said as we walked up the long, switch-backed ramp to board the ship. "I didn't even think of that." In fact, I'd purposefully avoided calling to tell her that I was no longer bringing my boyfriend with me. Now I felt guilty for inadvertently putting that news on Josh's shoulders.

"No problem. That's what friends are for." He threw me a playful grin. "And I'll be expecting a pretty amazing Christmas present this year."

"Roger that." He did deserve something big, and I had no idea what. I hadn't expected to see him till after the holiday, so my plan had been to buy him something on the cruise. Now my plan was to buy him something amazing on the cruise. There better be good shopping in St. Maarten.

As we boarded the Treasure of the Seas, we were funneled into a breathtaking multi-story atrium. The glass windows on either side of the ship extended all the way up to the open air of the top deck, and each deck from the bottom to the top had a lounge area overlooking the middle of the ship. Right in front of the glass elevators next to a grand glass staircase stood the tallest Christmas tree I'd ever seen. With the tropical daylight streaming through all the windows, it twinkled marvelously.

"Whoa," I said. "That is gorgeous."

"And you were afraid it wouldn't be Christmassy." Josh nudged my shoulder with his.

"Fine. It's a little Christmassy, but I still don't understand why Mom wants to spend Christmas in the tropics. There won't be any snow."

"There won't be snow in Austin either."

"Don't be so sensible," I told him. "If we are going on vacation anyway, we could have rented a mountain cabin or something someplace snowy. What's wrong with Colorado?"

But I knew that answer as soon as the words left my lips. My most recent ex was headed to Colorado. That's what was wrong with it. Maybe this tropical family getaway had saved me some very awkward run-ins with Shayne and Willow.

"Take your picture?" a photographer in a Cherish Cruises uniform asked us as she pointed to the tree where other passengers were smiling for another camera.

"Of course." Josh pulled me over in front of the tree and slung his arm over my shoulder. He tickled my side to get me to really smile, and the photographer snapped the picture right then.

She handed me an instant print from the camera and told us we could purchase the larger version in the photo gallery for framing. Then she wished us a Merry Christmas and moved on to the next passengers.

"You are so goofy," I said.

"What? I don't want mopey pictures to remember this vacation by," he said.

We did look happy in the picture. My nose was scrunched up in laughter, and his wide grin was directed at me, not the camera. I held the photo dramatically to my chest. "I'll treasure it forever."

"I'd expect nothing less."

I pulled out my phone to text Mom and tell her we'd made it onboard and were ready to start this Greyson family vacation, but before my thumbs could type a letter, I heard my brother's voice call my name.

~ 3 ~

NEW TRADITIONS

CHRIS WAVED AS he skirted around the other boarding passengers and made his way over to us from the Atrium Bar opposite the Christmas tree. My brother was as tall as Josh, but where Josh was lean and fit from kayaking in his free time, Chris was developing that businessman's belly from dedicating all his time to moving up at the office. He'd traded his usual tailored suit for chinos and a baby blue button-up, but he still looked way more formal than we did. I'd thrown on a comfy patchwork sundress for travel, and Josh wore his everyday jeans and t-shirt. Chris didn't care how casual we looked though. He wrapped me in a big bear hug. Then he shook Josh's hand and slapped him on the shoulder in that bro-hug way that guys always have. "Good to see you, man. Glad you could come."

"Likewise," Josh said. "Happy to be here."

I was happy that they both genuinely meant those things. Although they'd never hung out a lot, since

Chris was five years older than us, Josh and Chris had always gotten along well. They were both easy going, and they both had a head for business that I would never understand. Also, since Josh had never been my boyfriend, Chris had never given him the overprotective big brother act. If it were just the three of us this week, it would actually be a fun vacation. I really liked Chris when my parents weren't touting his successes at every turn, but they were bound to be here somewhere.

I glanced around nervously. "Where's everyone else?"

"They hit the buffet upstairs," Chris explained. "I thought I'd grab a beer and wait for you guys. I can only take so much of Jacob spouting useless knowledge. I'm trying to limit my exposure so I can survive the week with him."

"Good plan," I said.

Our sister, Amy, had married a guy who always knew more than you did about anything and wasn't afraid to tell you that. He'd managed to come across as very full of himself at every family function since he'd entered our lives a couple years ago. Chris and I had been sure he wouldn't last long, but then Amy had married him last summer and made him a permanent addition to our family. We were still adjusting.

"We can go catch up with them if you want," Chris offered. "I know Mom is anxious to see you."

I knew exactly why. She would want to ask about Shayne. "I don't think I'm ready for that."

"Let's check out some of the famous Cherish Cruises cocktails then." Josh motioned toward the bar.

"Are they famous?" Chris asked.

"Yeah, they have themed drinks every day," Josh said, leading the way to the bar.

"How do you know so much about cruising?" I asked.

Josh shrugged. "I read up on the cruiser boards online this morning."

"Of course you did," I said.

"A guy needs to know what he's in for," Josh said.

"True words," Chris agreed as we nabbed the last three stools at the Atrium Bar.

Behind the bar, glass shelves were set into a wide mirror that reflected the twinkling lights of the Christmas tree behind us along with the afternoon sun beaming in the atrium windows. The bar itself was inlaid with colorful resin swirls, and smaller Christmas trees, drizzled in fake snow, sat at each end of it, lending another touch of cheer to the space. If I hadn't been so apprehensive about meeting up with my family, I might have started to enjoy the trip the moment we walked aboard. Something about the elegant decorations and the ship filling with merry people made Christmas cruising feel a little bit magical.

The bartender, Antonio, added to the ambiance by welcoming us heartily and serving us drinks of the day, Frosty Mornings, which were deliciously sweet. Licking the sugar-coated rim made me feel like a kid. Maybe this week wouldn't be so bad once I got past the initial embarrassment of another failed relationship. I could sip candy concoctions poolside while my parents passed concerned glances my way.

"Will your family be missing you this week?" Chris asked Josh.

"Yeah. But they were very understanding," Josh said. "They love Kate, and I told them how important this week was to her."

That doubled my guilt at dragging Josh along. Family had always been important to him, and because of me, he was going to miss out on his mom's traditional Christmas brunch and game night with his nephews and all the other special moments with his family this week.

I loved how his mom always went all out for Christmas. She insisted on a live Douglas fir tree, decorated with hand-strung popcorn and multi-colored lights, and she baked for almost the entire month of December. Her house smelled like a sugar-filled pine forest this time of year.

"I'm sorry I pulled you away," I said.

"You guys are like my second family," Josh said. "And besides, I've been to Mom's Christmas brunch almost every year of my life. I've never taken a cruise for Christmas."

"To new traditions," my brother toasted.

We drank to that, and I silently hoped the abundance of Christmas cheer had a chance at balancing out my self-doubt this week.

Chris quickly dashed that hope by asking, "So, are you going to tell me what happened to this Shayne guy you were supposed to bring along?"

"I don't want to talk about it."

"All right. None of my business, but you know Mom's going to want the whole story."

"Oh, don't I know it." I sighed. "I guess the short of it is it turned out that he was not the guy I thought he was."

Chris patted my arm. "You know, it's totally okay that he wasn't the one, right? You'll find the right one."

"That's what I told her," Josh chimed in.

"Great minds think alike." Chris clinked glasses with Josh.

I huffed. "That's easy for you to say. Mom and Dad don't care if you ever get married. You are the perfect son already."

Chris laughed, but he didn't deny it. Because we all knew it was true.

~ 4 ~

A ROOM FOR ONE

BY THE TIME we finished a couple of Frosty Mornings in the atrium, it was time to line up for the muster drill. Thankfully that would take the initial stress out of meeting up with the rest of the family since we'd be on deck together with all of the other passengers onboard. There'd be no time for prying conversations about my love life yet.

As the alarm clanged to signal the start of the drill, the ship's staff directed us toward our designated meeting points on a lower outside deck of the ship. Because the family's rooms were all clustered together, we'd been assigned the same muster station and found each other there. With the crowd on the deck, we only had time for hasty hugs and hellos.

My sister, Amy, positively glowed. Apparently, marriage agreed with her. Her blonde hair glistened in the sun, and her cheeks already looked sun-kissed. I'd never know how she found the time to accomplish so much and look so perfect doing it. She hugged me tight.

"We wondered when you would show up. I was afraid you'd miss the boat." Typical Amy, she managed to sound concerned and condescending in the same breath. Almost without fail, the older sister in her doubted my abilities to adult on my own, but I had done little in life to prove her wrong, so maybe her concern wasn't misplaced.

She passed me on to Mom, who gave me a sympathetic smile as she wrapped her arms around me. Her flowery perfume overwhelmed me as she whispered in my ear, "We'll talk later."

I began dreading that immediately.

Dad gave me a warm hug, and I complimented his new salt and pepper beard. Retirement had definitely relaxed him.

Jacob, my sister's husband, was the last one I got to. We had an awkward almost handshake, half-hug. He seemed more nervous than usual and rattled off obscure facts about cruise ship tonnage as Josh and I settled in beside him to listen to Captain Karlsson's announcements over the loudspeaker.

The captain welcomed us aboard and wished us all a merry holiday cruise. Then he explained how the boats hanging over our heads on this deck would be our life rafts in the case of an emergency. I looked up at them longingly and wondered if they could also be used as an escape raft in the event of a personal meltdown due to family pressures.

Josh elbowed my side. "Don't even think about it."

How did he know? I crossed my arms over my chest and waited for the end of the announcements.

With our mandatory safety drill done, Mom insisted we all find our rooms so we could unpack and freshen up before meeting for dinner. I was thankful for the time to relax for a few before we began what I assumed would be a whirlwind of activities that she'd have planned for us for the week.

As we walked up the few flights of stairs to our rooms, everyone kept the conversation light, talking about their flights in and the beautiful weather. We all followed Mom's lead down a long curved hallway to our rooms. She and Dad stopped first. Next to them was Amy and Jacob's room. Then Josh and Chris. Then me. Always the last one. Always alone.

I used my keycard to open the door, and the view took my breath away. The room looked like any luxury hotel room might. There was a plush bed with plenty of fluffy pillows, opposite a wall of mirrors above a desk and drawers. But the view through the sliding glass doors to a private balcony was nothing but blue skies over Biscayne Bay. I let my room door swing shut behind me and went straight to the balcony.

Stepping out into the warm Miami day, I breathed in the fresh ocean breeze and leaned onto the rail. I closed my eyes for a while, soaking in the peace of the afternoon and the gentle rocking of the ship as it pushed away from the dock. I might have stood there all afternoon if the balcony partition hadn't rattled beside me and made me jump.

My heart quickened as I grabbed the railing to steady myself. "What the—"

"Kate, are you over there?" Josh's voice came from the other side of the balcony wall.

"Oh my gosh, you scared me."

"Sorry. Didn't mean to. I was working on this partition. I think we can open this pass through and have twice the balcony space. Can you reach your unlock lever at the top of the door?"

I looked up to see a lever right at the edge of my reach. I strained up on my tiptoes and clicked it open. The wall that had been separating our balconies swung toward Josh and smacked him right in the face.

"Ouch." He rubbed his nose as he caught the door in his other hand, folded it back, and reattached it in the open position.

"Sorry," I said. "Come on over. I'll get you some ice."

He followed me back into my room and leaned onto the desk to examine his face in the mirror. "I'm glad we took that picture by the tree earlier. This might bruise."

I pulled the picture out of my dress pocket and tucked it into the corner of the mirror. "Good thing I have something to remember your previously handsome days by."

He sat down at the desk and rocked the chair back on two legs. "Good thing."

I got some ice out of the mini-fridge and wrapped it in a towel for him to hold against his nose. I really hoped I hadn't given him a black eye for Christmas. I felt bad enough about him sacrificing his holiday for me already.

"Are you going to be okay rooming with Chris for the week?" I asked.

"Sure. We've known each other forever, and he seems relieved that he's not stuck rooming with a stranger."

That was one benefit of bringing Josh instead of Shayne. My family already loved Josh. He'd fit right in without any of that awkwardness we all felt with my sister's husband. I'd hoped my family would have loved Shayne, but you never know. My brother would have tolerated him for me, but Chris's usual social circles did not include guys who taught yoga. His friends tended toward the suit and tie variety.

A knock sounded at the door, and I went to answer it, expecting it to be luggage delivery. To my surprise, Mom was standing there. She'd already changed from her travel clothes into a plaid skirt suit for dinner. It was a casual look on her, but it was probably nicer than anything I owned. Every hair in her short dark bob was perfectly in place, and her makeup tastefully accentuated her high cheekbones and her light eyes.

"Is your room all right?" she asked.

"Uh, yeah. It's great in here. Thank you so much. That view is amazing. I didn't expect anything like this."

"I wanted to make sure you were okay," she said with her special brand of prying concern.

Great. Here we go. The conversation I couldn't avoid. I would have to tell her all about how Shayne had unceremoniously left me for a fellow instructor. How, unlike her other children, I could not hang onto a stable relationship or a reliable career. I opened the door wider, so she could come in, but she paused when she saw Josh sitting with his feet up on the desk.

"Oh, I didn't realize Josh was here," she said, surprise in her voice.

"Hey, Kim." He waved at her with one hand while the other held the icy towel on his face.

"Yeah, he bonked his nose on the balcony," I explained. "I got him some ice."

"Oh dear. Are you all right, Josh?" she asked.

"I'm sure I'll be right as rain by dinner," he assured her.

"Well, don't let me interrupt." A hint of a smile crossed her face. "We'll meet in the dining room at six." With that, she backed away and went back to her room.

"That was weird," Josh said as I closed the door.

"I'll say. I was sure she had come over to hash out my failed loved life."

"Now, she'll have to wait until dinner."

I ran my hands through my hair. He was right. Turning her away now would make dinner that much more humiliating. I would have to talk about breaking up with Shayne with the whole family. Likely right after my sister told some story about her latest heroic exploits in the ER.

"Great," I said. "Can't wait for that."

~ 5 ~

To the Happy Couple

I COULDN'T STOP fidgeting with my bracelet as Josh and I walked to the dining room. The rough cut aquamarine stone strung around my wrist with braided leather was one of my favorites, a present from Josh when I'd finished my yoga instructor training. It was supposed to promote feelings of peace and tranquility for the wearer. It was not working tonight. All the stone was doing tonight was adding a nice accent to my blue maxi dress.

Josh noticed my restless hands. "You are going to be fine. I'll be right there with you, and you don't have to talk about Shayne if you don't want to."

"She's going to ask."

"She will, but only because she cares about you. She wants you to be happy."

I nodded. That was partially true. She wanted me to be happy on the normal life path that her other children were on. I was sure she'd never be satisfied with my current direction.

I wasn't. I didn't want to turn thirty next year still single with no real plan for opening my own studio someday. But the stark reality was that I had no prospects for either of those things. It was like I'd spent my entire adult life running in place so far.

At the dining room entrance, we were greeted by a smiling hostess in a blue and pink button-up shirt dress, a more feminine version of the usual Cherish Cruises polo and trousers we'd seen other staffers in. "Welcome to the Golden Pearl dining room. May I show you to your table?"

She led us into a two-story dining room ringed with floor to ceiling windows that overlooked the ocean. The crystal chandeliers and mahogany banisters made me feel like I'd been transported straight into a scene from *Titanic*. A grand marble staircase led up to the second floor, but we passed it by for a large round table behind it near the windows where the rest of my family was already seated, looking over their menus.

Our waiter, an energetic guy named Tristan, and his equally enthusiastic assistant Jerome, came for our drink order almost as soon as we sat down. Dad ordered a couple bottles of wine for the table, which I was thankful for. I'd never picked up his discerning taste for wine. Probably because my budget never allowed for anything more than the sale items at the bodega down the street from my apartment.

Mom asked about Josh's nose, and he proudly displayed a bruise-free face, but then everyone had to hear the story about how I'd knocked the balcony partition into his face. Chris had already heard the story once, but he still found it hilarious and laughed harder than anyone else. Dad said that no one should underestimate the strength of a yoga instructor. At least I could provide the comic relief on this vacation if nothing else.

Before I'd had time to decide what to order for dinner, Tristan returned with our wine and started filling our glasses. My sister tried to discreetly say, "None for me," but Mom and I both noticed and gave her curious looks.

Amy waited until all our glasses were full and then made her announcement. "Jacob and I have news," she started to get everyone's attention. Once the guys had looked up from their menus, she continued, "We are expecting."

Mom squealed as only a first-time grandmother can. Chris clapped Jacob on the back, and Dad offered a toast to the new addition to the family. I jumped up to give Amy and Jacob a hug and my heartfelt congratulations. I couldn't help but be happy for my sister and her overly perfect life no matter how much I didn't like living in its shadow.

We settled back down and learned that she was sixteen weeks along, so she was due in June. Then she told us her plans to cut back at work and talked about finding good preschools near their home in Dallas. In the ever-practical Amy style, every meticulous detail was considered and decided with efficiency. By the time we'd ordered and eaten our appetizers, the kid's whole life was planned out. I silently hoped he or she could live up to those expectations better than I had. At least they could commiserate with their Auntie Kate if they didn't.

Once dinner arrived, my brother decided it was time to share his news. "You're looking at the new Vice President of Sales for the entire North American region."

That earned him a round of congratulations and questions about his new responsibilities. He gladly told us about his new corner office that came with a nice bump in salary, so he could finally ink the deal on that condo he'd been eyeing in Manhattan. Chris deserved every bit of his success. He'd worked hard for it, and I was proud of him. When I told him so, he gave me a sincere, "Thanks, Katie," that warmed my heart.

I wished I had anything to share that would make him proud of me. And as though Mom could read those thoughts, her pitying gaze landed on me. She knew as well as everyone else at the table that I didn't have any revelatory news. I still taught at the same yoga studio. I still lived with the same roommate I'd had for the past five years. And I once again did not even have a serious boyfriend. I'd never felt more like

I didn't belong in this family than I did right then. I twirled my spoon through the layers of the trifle in front of me, but I didn't want dessert. I wanted to crawl under the table and disappear.

Mom glanced away from me as she said, "It's wonderful to have the whole family together to celebrate these milestones with each other."

At first I was relieved that she wasn't going to bring up my humiliating breakup in the middle of the dinner that had so far been about celebrating my siblings' successes, but then a wave of irritation rushed over me.

I'd gotten overlooked my entire life. Maybe because my brother and sister always did everything first since they were older, and they always set a high bar to be measured against. My sister had gone to medical school. My brother had gotten an MBA. What had I done? I got certified as a yoga instructor. My sister had moved to Dallas. My brother was now moving to Manhattan. I had moved right back to Austin and stayed there in a tiny apartment across town from where I'd grown up. I wanted for once in my life to prove that I was worthy of my parents' praise and attention too.

"I have news," I blurted out before I could think better of it.

All eyes turned to me, and I'm sure I turned seven shades of red. I wasn't used to my family giving me that much attention, ever. Now I had to come up with something good to say. But what could that possibly be?

"You do?" Mom perked up with a curious half-smile.

What did she think I was about to say? What kind of expectations did she have for my life by now? I'd seen that same look on her face earlier today—when she'd seen Josh in my room unexpectedly. Did she think something was happening between him and me? I looked instinctively to him. He had his I-hope-you-know-what-you're-doing face on.

I didn't know what I was doing at all.

"Katie?" Dad prodded.

I said the first thing that popped into my head as I stared into Josh's sweet brown eyes. "I'm going to marry Josh."

Josh's mouth slipped open in a second of befuddlement that mirrored my own, and I'm sure we were both thinking the exact same thing—*Why on earth did I say that?*

Josh recovered almost instantly with a broad grin as my family all started talking at once. Was he already picturing laughing about this mortifying moment a few years down the line? *Remember that time you tried to tell your parents we were engaged? Who would believe that?*

No one was going to believe it. Josh dated serious, successful women, and I dated flaky musicians most of the time. Our tastes were totally opposite, which is part of what made us such great friends—we balanced each other out. But moving from great friends to engaged couple was a giant implausible leap.

When I looked away from Josh, I expected to see the family laughing at me like I'd told a bad joke, but Mom had gotten up and come over to throw her arms around my neck. Then she took Josh's face in both her hands and said, "You've made me the happiest mother in the world." She kissed each of his cheeks.

Josh laughed nervously and thanked her as everyone else was hugging me and saying congratulations and echoing her sentiments.

"Glad you guys finally realized you're perfect for each other," Chris said. "I can't believe you didn't tell me this afternoon. You really had me going with all that talk about not finding the right guy."

"Yeah, right?" I managed a weak laugh.

Chris thought we were perfect for each other? What was happening? My family was believing this.

The waiter came over to see what the commotion was, and Dad ordered champagne for us and the three surrounding tables. Once everyone had champagne in hand, he stood up and said, "To my youngest daughter, who has found the love of her life. May their friendship that has blossomed into love carry them on their journey together for the rest of their days."

Everyone toasted and cheered. I thought I might pass out.

Josh seemed to sense that. He threw a supportive arm around my shoulders and kissed my forehead as I leaned into him. I teared up. I was so going to hell for this. I had just told a really big fat lie to my entire family and all of the strangers eating dinner around us. I had no idea how to get out of this now. I needed to think fast, but the questions didn't stop. There was no time to think.

"Let's see the ring," my sister said as everyone settled back into their chairs.

"Oh." I hesitated as I hid my bare hand under the table. I had not thought this through at all. There was no ring. Because we weren't engaged. Could I come out and say that right now? Like, *LOL, thought you guys would get a kick out of that. Just kidding.*

Josh took my hand in both of his and improvised for me. "We were hoping to pick one out on this trip. It was all so spur of the moment. I mean, I looked at her one day and said that's the woman I'm going to marry, and I had to ask her right that minute. Just like that. Without any planning or anything."

"That's so romantic," Mom said. "Where were you?"

I looked desperately to Josh. Were we really going with this? And if so, where would he have proposed?

And when? This was one lie stacked on another—an awful lie trifle, and I was fresh out of berries.

Josh, however, seemed to have a basketful. He gazed lovingly at me, and as though reminiscing about a fond memory we shared, he came out with, "On Lady Bird Lake trail. We'd gone for a sunset walk, and the last rays of the day were shining in her hair, and I knew it was the perfect moment." He turned to the others then and continued, "I got down on one knee and asked Kate to be my wife."

"Oh my gosh," my sister cooed. She held her hands to her heart like Josh had tugged at every heartstring.

Mom looked completely starry-eyed.

They were buying this charade, and Josh was playing the role of a doting fiancé like he was born to it. I should have expected that. He was a romantic at heart. He might be all laid-back and playful on the outside, but on the inside, he was as mushy as Nicholas Sparks. I'd seen that tender side on full display with his past girlfriends. Now those charms were working in my favor, but that couldn't last long. Because this wasn't real. I had made it up and probably ruined whatever good graces were left for me with my parents. I hoped I hadn't ruined my friendship with Josh. Would he hate me for this later or find it endlessly amusing?

I stewed in that worry while everyone else ate their dessert and continued toasting "to the happy couple." As the excitement died down and the dining room started to clear out, Josh found a lull in the conversation to suggest to me, "I thought we might take a walk under the stars, Sugar Bean."

I winced at the absurd nickname. He was going to make me pay for this big time, and then he may never speak to me again. What kind of horrible best friend had I turned into, dragging him into a last-minute Christmas vacation with my family and then putting him on the spot like that?

I smiled sweetly and said, "That sounds wonderful."

No time like the present for a leisurely stroll around deck and a what-the-hell-did-you-just-do conversation.

~ 6 ~

THE RIGHT THING

JOSH PRACTICALLY JOGGED up the stairs to the top deck. A brisk wind pushed back at us, but that didn't stop him from walking halfway around the ship to the dimly lit aft overlook. I kept pace behind him and braced myself for the rebuke I deserved. He stopped at the back railing and made sure we were the only people fool enough to take a late evening walk in the gusting wind before he asked the obvious question, "What are you doing?"

"I panicked. Please don't hate me," I begged as I tied my hair back into a ponytail so it would stop whipping into my mouth.

He ran his hands over his face in exasperation. "I don't hate you, but I'm extremely confused right now. There was nothing to panic about at dinner. Certainly no cause for that kind of drastic action. Everything was going fine. We'd made it all the way to dessert. I don't even think your mom was going to bring your love life up. She was too excited about Amy and

Chris. But you couldn't leave well enough alone, and you felt the need to drag me down with you. What did you expect me to do?"

He'd known me long enough to know that conversation at dinner had pushed all of my buttons, but I'd surprised us both with that engagement announcement.

"I don't know. It's not like this was a well thought out plan. I didn't expect you to do anything because I didn't know I was going to say that. I just lost it. I couldn't sit there and live with the fact that I had nothing to contribute. Mom and Dad were so ecstatic about Amy's baby and Chris's amazing promotion, and there I was with nothing to say. Like always. Mom gave me that pitying look and then moved right on celebrating her two kids that amount to something."

Josh softened and laid a sympathetic hand on my arm. "I've never understood this inferiority complex. No one is judging you but yourself. Those people love you. And they love you for who you are. They don't want you to be anybody else."

I scoffed at that thought. "Well, they seemed to love us both a lot more when they thought we were engaged. My dad actually teared up with pride during his toast."

"Okay, I'll give you that." Josh nodded. "Your mom has definitely never double kissed my cheeks before. Not even when I saved you from that horrible prom date senior year. That was a total new one tonight."

"Right?" I said hopefully. He was going to see my side of this and help me figure out what to do next.

"But that doesn't make it any better. If anything, it makes it worse. Once they find out it was all a lie, they are going to hate me. Why did you have to say that? You couldn't have picked something a little more innocuous to lie about?"

I rubbed at my temples as though I could retroactively rub some sense into my head. "Maybe if I'd had time to think. But Mom was looking at me, and then I was looking at you, and I said the first thing that popped into my head."

Josh's lips quirked in amusement. "The first thing you think about when you look at me is that you're going to marry me? That takes this friendship to a whole new level."

"Be serious, Josh."

"Okay, table that. In all seriousness, what is going on with you? I've never seen you this insecure before. So Shayne wasn't the right guy. There have been other wrong guys, and none of them made you this crazy."

I blew out a long breath and confessed the thing I hadn't dared say out loud to anyone. "I thought he might propose this week, but instead he left me for someone else right before Christmas."

"Oh, Kate," Josh said softly, finally understanding the whole picture. "That's why you were so excited about bringing him."

"And then we get here, and Amy is so happily married and having a baby, and Chris is conquering the world, and I haven't moved forward in like seven years. Life is starting to pass me by. I'm not doing anything I'm supposed to be doing."

Josh laid his hands on my shoulders and made me meet his eyes. "You have to live on your own timeline. Nobody else's. You're putting too much pressure on yourself."

I chewed on my bottom lip. It was not my imagination that I'd spent a lifetime being held up to compare to my older brother and sister. I had always fallen short. That's why I felt so much pressure now. It'd been mounting for nearly thirty years. Josh couldn't understand. His parents had always been proud of him.

"You don't understand," I protested weakly.

"We've been friends so long. Walk me through it, and we'll find our way out of this."

I trusted that he meant that. As wretched as I felt about the night, I took some solace in the fact that he wasn't throwing in the towel on our friendship because I'd made a total idiot move and wrapped him up in a lie in front of my entire family.

"At dinner, I was thinking..." I had no idea what I was thinking. How could I explain my momentary insanity? I took a deep breath and thought back to that moment. To mom's curious smile when I'd said I had news. "I was thinking how surprised Mom was to see you in my room this afternoon and that maybe she thought something was going on between us. And then I guess my mind skipped from that to Shayne."

"Thinking about other guys already. Our marriage may be doomed." Josh stuck his lip out in exaggerated disappointment.

I ignored his attempted humor and continued, "I mean, I guess the wished-for proposal was still in my head, and it came out of my mouth before I had time to stop it."

He sighed.

"I didn't mean to do this, Josh."

"Well, it's done now, so let's figure out our next move." He turned toward the dark ocean as if it might offer some answers.

"Yes. Good idea. Any idea what that next move should be?"

"You're the one with all the creative ideas tonight."

We both leaned on the rail and thought in silence. There wasn't a cloud in the moonless sky, so we could see all the stars. It was a beautiful night to feel so bad. There had to be something we could do that would make all this feel better.

"What if we stay pretend engaged?" I suggested. That seemed like the easiest way out for the time being. "We ride the week out as is."

That earned me a skeptical brow. "You want to lie to your family for the entire Christmas vacation?"

No. I did not want to do that, but our choices were limited here. "Yes?"

"And then what? Where does that end?"

"Um, well, we break up when we get back home."

"And we stay best friends? I don't think your family is going to want me in your life if I go breaking your heart." He nudged my shoulder with his.

"We're going to have to break up at some point," I argued. "If we do it this week with all of them around, it will be incredibly awkward, and they'll ask a ton of questions. I mean, you're rooming with my brother."

"Yeah, I don't like the breakup option," Josh said.

"Well, we can't stay together forever. That would put a damper on our dating lives, don't you think?"

"It would if either of us had a dating life." Josh laughed.

"Ouch," I said.

"Too soon?"

"A little bit."

He wrapped his arm around my shoulders. "Sorry."

I laid my head against him. "You're forgiven if you come up with a good plan to get us out of this."

He squeezed me tighter for a second, and then he said the thing I didn't want him to say. "We tell the truth. Isn't that one of your principles of yoga? Be true to yourself and others?"

That was not the answer I was looking for. I pushed out of his arms. "You choose now to start listening to my advice?"

He grinned. "I always listen to you."

I rolled my eyes. "Don't be charming."

"Seriously, we tell your family that it was all a big misunderstanding. That we got carried away in the moment. It was meant to get a laugh, and we took it too far."

Josh always made so much sense. I really disliked that sometimes.

"I can't do that." The thought of looking into my family's faces tomorrow and telling them that I had lied to them tonight made me sick to my stomach.

"You can," Josh said. "You are a good person, who sometimes does inexplicable things. But deep down, you are a remarkable, caring woman. They know all of that about you. They will accept that you made a mistake."

"And that you were my unwitting co-conspirator?" That was the last card I had to play, appealing to any need he might feel to preserve his reputation with my family.

He didn't go for it. "I may not be welcome at Christmas dinner this week, but I'm sure they will understand. Eventually."

"Okay," I agreed. "In the morning, I'll tell them. I'll take all the heat for it. I'll tell them it was all my fault."

"I'll be right there with you, and I at least get partial blame for blowing it out of proportion. It's the right thing to do."

"That doesn't make it any easier." I exhaled a shaky breath.

He pulled me in for another comforting hug.

I rested my head on his shoulder and whispered, "I'm sorry I messed this up."

"It's going to be okay," he promised.

~ 7 ~

BREAKFAST SURPRISE

THE NEXT MORNING, I hurried to breakfast in the dining room. Back to the scene of the crime. I hadn't meant to be late, but after I'd done my usual Sun Salutations to settle myself for the morning, I'd spent too long deciding which sundress would make me look the most forgivable. Eventually, I'd thrown on my favorite yellow one dotted with white daisies. It was the most comfortable, and I reasoned that I might as well feel good in my clothes because that was the only thing I was going to feel good about today. I had never dreaded anything so much in my life as telling my family that I had made up the whole engagement with Josh last night so they would think more of me.

This even ranked above the time when I was twelve years old, and I had to admit that it was my fault our dog Muffin had gotten out and gone missing for a week. I'd accidentally left the back gate open when I'd snuck out to a friend's house to watch HBO. The guilt had been too much to bear. Of course, right as I tearfully confessed to leaving the gate open, Muffin wandered back into the yard. This time, unfortunately, there was no possible happy ending for the confession I was about to make. There was no getting this dog back inside the gate.

The same hostess greeted me with an overabundance of cheer for this early in the day and showed me to our table. In the morning light, the dining room looked too grand for a simple breakfast, but I supposed it made a nice dramatic backdrop for revealing the truth about Josh and me. The rest of my family was already seated and chatting over their coffee, including Josh, who stood to pull out my chair for me. He whispered an unsettling, "We need to talk," in my ear as I sat down.

Before I had time to fully register that, Mom started in with, "Kate, we were talking about plans for the day."

"I've already signed us up for the gingerbread house decorating contest," Amy said. "With your art skills, our family will be a shoo-in."

"Sounds great," I said offhandedly while my mind backtracked to Josh's comment. What did we need to talk about? What had happened in the five minutes before I got here? I took a long sip of water as if that would do anything to boost my courage for what I knew I needed to say to the family.

"Then maybe we could hit the pool deck," Chris suggested. "I mean, why take a Christmas cruise if not to enjoy the sunshine."

Mom and Amy agreed that relaxing by the pool sounded like the perfect afternoon. I nodded along as I watched the waiter fill my coffee. I couldn't be expected to come clean without a little caffeine in my system.

"First," Mom said, "we have a surprise for you two."

Josh nudged my knee under the table, and I spilled way too much sugar in my coffee. I looked up to realize she was talking to us.

"Oh, about that." I cleared my throat.

Mom waved away whatever she thought my protest might be. "We know you aren't one to like a fuss made over you, but your father and I were so delighted to hear your engagement news last night. We are grateful that you two finally found love together after it has obviously been stirring between you for many years."

Under any other circumstances, I would have welcomed the attention from my mom. That's what had prompted me to make up the engagement in the first place. But this was all wrong. She thought love had been stirring between Josh and me for years? I threw Josh a questioning glance. He lifted a subtle, don't-ask-me shoulder and kept his attention on my mom.

She continued, "Josh has been part of our lives for such a long time, we feel like he's already family, but we want to officially welcome him as our future son-in-law. We got you all an engagement present."

My throat went dry. I tried to soothe it with a drink of coffee but choked on the overly sweet concoction I'd created.

Josh patted me on the back as I did my best to hide behind my napkin.

"Are you okay?" He was definitely asking about more than the coughing, but there was no way to communicate the panic rising in my chest.

I just nodded as I dropped the napkin back to my lap. I couldn't hide from this. I had to come clean with them now before this got any farther out of hand.

Before I had a chance, Dad started in, "Your mom and I are overjoyed to see our little girl happy. The way you and Josh light up for each other, it reminds us what it was like to be young and in love." He squeezed Mom's hand. "You deserve all the joy you've found together, and we want to celebrate that with you."

Josh and I lit up with joy for each other? We must have been much more convincing than I'd felt at dinner last night. Or everyone had had too much champagne.

"That's so nice of you," I said. My parents were genuinely the nicest people. What had I been thinking lying to them about something as important as getting engaged? And to Josh! They had always loved him as my best friend. I hoped they would understand that he'd been acting as the best friend in the world when he'd covered for me last night. I had to make sure they wouldn't hold this against him. Even if they held it against me. "I can't accept anything."

"Nonsense," Dad said. "You have to let us celebrate you. We won't take no for an answer. We've made reservations for the entire family at the exclusive Chef's Supper for Christmas dinner."

My sister gasped. "It's supposed to be to die for." Her eyes were twinkling with dreams of a fantastic feast. Probably because she was now eating for two.

"An awesome way to celebrate you guys together for Christmas," my brother piped in.

My heart sank. I was about to ruin the entire week. I might as well get it over with. "I, uh..." I couldn't think exactly how to blurt it out. I'd practiced this all morning long, and there was no way to say it without sounding pathetic, and slightly unhinged.

Josh placed his warm hand over mine on the table and tightened my fingers in his. I thought he was giving me some encouragement. Then he spoke for us, "Thank you all. That's so generous. I think you've made Kate speechless for the first time in her life." That got a chuckle from everyone. Then he went on,

"We are excited to celebrate with you this week. Isn't that right, Honey Bear?"

Was he really willing to continue this charade? Christmas was at the end of the week. Could we lie to them till then? He'd pretty much argued that that was the worst idea ever last night. Why would he change his mind now?

Josh leaned over and planted a kiss on my cheek, and I gave him a small, confused smile.

Mom apparently took that as my assent. She clapped her hands together and said, "Excellent," as though that were the final word on the matter. Then everyone went back to planning the day ahead.

I spent the rest of breakfast staring out at the blue ocean, half-listening to my family chatter on about what they wanted to see and do this week and half-wondering why Josh hadn't let me confess. He really should have stuck to the plan. That was our one chance to correct course. Now we'd sailed our ship of lies into deep waters and left our life-raft back onshore.

~ 8 ~

LITTLE PINK GINGERBREAD HOUSES

JOSH AND I lingered at the breakfast table as everyone else excused themselves to get ready for the day. Amy told me more than twice to meet up at the Atrium Bar for the gingerbread house decorating contest at eleven. I assured her we could hardly wait and then watched her and Jacob make their way out of the dining room.

Finally alone, I turned to Josh. "Want to tell me what that was about? I thought you'd made it pretty clear last night that continuing this fake engagement was not a good idea. I seem to remember some noble ideas you had about the right thing to do."

He fidgeted with his empty coffee cup and refused to look at me. "Oh, I remember."

"What happened then?"

"Katie." He only called me that when he really wanted something. I'd grown out of the Katie phase of my name in college when I wanted to prove to the world that I could be taken seriously. "I couldn't look them in the eyes this morning and break their hearts, and I couldn't let you do it either. They are over the moon about this. Chris couldn't talk about anything else when I got back to the room last night. He went on and on about how he always knew we would end up together and how he thought I was the perfect guy for you. He actually said, 'If I could pick anyone out to make my sister happy, it would be you.'"

"He said that?"

Chris always found a fault with every guy I'd ever dated. His unconditional approval of Josh marrying me was something for the record books.

"He did. And this morning, they were nothing but smiles when Chris and I got here. Your mom and sister were giving me instructions on how to buy you the perfect engagement ring. Then when your dad said they wanted to take us out to celebrate for Christmas and welcome me to the family, the hurt look on your face was too much. I could see that family acceptance you wanted slipping right through your fingers because I told you we had to be scrupulous about this whole thing. I couldn't do that to you. It's worth one week of a guilty conscience. We will figure out how to get out of it once we get back home."

So much relief washed over me I threw my arms around Josh's neck and thanked him profusely. I'd been tied up in knots all night, and he'd just untangled them all for me. Well, except the one lie, but we could figure that out when we got home. Just like he said. "You are the absolute best friend a girl could ever ask for. You won't regret this."

"I'm sure I will. Soak it up while you can because once I fake break your heart, Chris may break me for real."

I waved that thought off. "Don't be dramatic. He's a total suit."

"Which means he could hire someone."

I laughed, but come to think of it, Chris really could. He had always been overprotective when it came to me and Amy. Josh and I would have to find a way to split amicably when this week was over.

And now we had time to come up with a really good breakup lie to cover up our engagement lie. Maybe we could even tell a version of the truth—like we realized we make better friends than life partners. We'd be able to let everyone down easy instead of blindsiding them with the news that none of this was real. That made me feel better about it all. Mostly.

JOSH AND I spent the next couple of hours hiding out at the empty English pub behind the casino rehearsing more of our engagement story. We decided that I had broken up with Shayne because he didn't feel like the one. I had a sixth sense about these things in our version of the story. Then Josh had taken the opportunity to finally ask me out, as he'd been pining to do for a while now. The pining was my idea. I argued that it gave our story verisimilitude. Josh rolled his eyes and said I could tell the story that way if I wanted, but there would be no pining in his version. Once we'd gone out on a date and finally saw each other as more than friends, we instantly fell in love and only had eyes for each other from that moment on. It had been such a whirlwind romance that we hadn't thought to tell anyone else until we got the entire family together for Christmas. We were satisfied that all of that sounded plausible, and at least we had something to say if anyone asked any more pressing questions about our relationship.

When we arrived in the atrium at a quarter till eleven, Amy and Jacob had already checked our gingerbread decorating team in and were arranging our supplies at one of the twenty tables spread between the bar and the giant Christmas tree.

Josh reached for my hand and locked his fingers through mine. "Let's take this show on the road, shall we?"

We walked hand in hand over to the table, and Amy greeted us with way more enthusiasm than anyone should rightly have about making a gingerbread house. She was taking family time super seriously now that she was starting her own.

"You're early," she said. "I like this Josh influence on you."

Jacob gave us a nod as he looked up from his clipboard, where he was dutifully checking off our gingerbread walls and candy canes and gumdrops and tubes of icing.

The rest of the family joined us by the time the cruise director, Nicole, a cheerful woman in cat-eye glasses, grabbed the mic at the Atrium Bar and announced the contest rules. "Each team has two hours to complete their gingerbread masterpiece with the materials given. Then the entries will be placed on display here in the atrium for the next few days for your fellow passengers to admire and vote on. Voting will end at sail away from St. Maarten. Votes will then be tallied, and the winners announced here at our tree trimming party on our next day at sea. The first three places will receive a Cherish Cruises winner's trophy, and, of course, gingerbread bragging rights." Nicole held up the trophy for all to see, a small pink stylized cruise ship riding blue waves.

"We definitely need that to take home," Josh said.

"Oh yeah," Chris agreed.

"All right, teams. Are you ready?" Nicole asked.

The crowd yelled, "Yes!"

"Then your time starts now!"

My entire family turned to me, and Amy asked, "All right, what's our game plan?"

"Oh, I'm in charge?" I asked, surprised.

"You're the artist," Chris said.

I wasn't sure enjoying painting in my spare time qualified me as an artist, but in the family's eyes, it did make me the creative one. I looked around and sized up the competition. Nineteen other groups of friends and families were all diving into their materials, pasting their gingerbread walls with icing to assemble their houses, and starting to argue over whether gumdrops or pretzels made better trees.

If we wanted to stand out, we needed to do something special. Ignoring the expectant stares of my family, I breathed in deep to clear my mind and felt the ship sway gently under my feet.

"I've got an idea," I said. I sketched out a design on the back of Jacob's checklist, and my family all agreed that it was an awesome idea. I listed off the things we'd need to do to get this thing built in our allotted time, and Jacob assigned everyone small tasks and kept track of our dwindling supplies as well as how quickly time was passing.

Jacob told us almost an hour had gone by before I looked up and took in the moment. Dad and Chris and Josh had sliced up our gingerbread walls to match my drawing, and Mom and Amy were gluing them together with our pink icing while I mixed some blue food coloring into more icing and slathered it on our base to hold our gingerbread sculpture in place. Everyone was talking and laughing as they worked, having a great time with it.

Josh glanced up and winked at me then. I gave him a genuine smile in return. Because of him this week was turning from the sorrowful disaster I'd feared into the dream family vacation my mom had wanted. I was lucky he'd come with me.

As the last minutes of the contest ticked by, we used every last piece of candy they had given us. We stood back and admired our handiwork—a beautiful gingerbread replica of our cruise ship, complete with gumdrop passengers on deck.

"Looks like a winner to me." Dad draped a proud arm around my shoulders.

"Great work, Honeybee." Josh gave me a high five, and then as if he remembered we were supposed to be engaged now, he kept my hand in his and brought it up to his lips for a kiss on my knuckles.

That chivalrous effort made me laugh. We'd have to work on our PDA. We had neglected to plan for any public displays of affection in our relationship plotting session this morning. No one in the family seemed to notice anything off about it though, so I breathed an inward sigh of relief and made a mental note to remember that I was supposed to be madly in love with Josh. I needed to act like it.

When Mom insisted we line up behind our masterpiece for a family photo, I pulled Josh's arms around my waist. He must have been thinking the same thing because he didn't pull away at all. He wrapped his arms naturally around me and leaned in as Mom handed her phone to a staff member who snapped a dozen pictures of us.

"Perfect," Mom exclaimed as she examined the photos on her phone. "Our first family photo of the week. I'm getting one of these framed."

That dampened my good spirits. By the time she got home and got that printed out, Josh and I would have found a way to break up.

I tried to push those thoughts aside as we wandered past the other contest entries on our way out of the atrium. Some of the gingerbread houses looked like they were about to fall apart and may not survive being moved to the display tables in front of the Christmas tree, but others looked pretty good. There must be some professional pastry chefs on board. Those people knew how to sculpt icing. Every one of them had made a traditional gingerbread house though. We were the only ones who had thought outside the box and made a cruise ship.

That worried me that I'd gone outside the bounds of the competition. Had they directed us to make a house specifically? I couldn't remember. My creativity might get us disqualified. But as the staff cleaned up the assembly tables and moved the houses in front of the tree for display, no one came to tell us our gingerbread cruise ship couldn't be judged, and no one tossed it in the trash. That had to be a good sign.

"We are definitely winning this," Chris said as he assessed the competition.

I wished I shared his confidence. I didn't want to let the family down any more than I was already going to when I told them Josh wasn't really joining the family.

~ 9 ~

THAT KIND OF SILLY

AFTER A DELICIOUS lunch at the buffet, where I managed to temporarily suppress my worries with a double scoop of strawberry gelato, we headed back to our rooms to change into swimsuits for our afternoon on the pool deck. I might prefer wintry Christmases, but I wasn't going to pass up the chance to lounge in the sun with a Christmas cocktail in my hand when the opportunity presented itself.

I threw on the red and green bikini I'd bought specially for this trip, and while I was rummaging around the bottom of my suitcase for my sun hat, I found the Christmas tree swim trunks I'd brought for Shayne. I'd thought that he'd think they were funny, and it would be cute to have couples swimwear. Now it was just sad. I'd already packed by the time he told me he wasn't coming, and I hadn't remembered to take them out of my suitcase with all the stress of leaving without him.

I sunk onto the bed with swim trunks in hand. What was I doing this week? I'd thought I might be getting engaged to my boyfriend, and instead I was pretending to be engaged to my best friend so my family would think better of me. My life was reaching new lows.

Tapping on the glass of my balcony door startled me, and I looked up to see Josh smiling in at me with a towel slung over his shoulder.

"Ready, Butter Bean?" he asked when I opened the door for him.

I smacked him with the shorts in my hand. "What is with the ridiculous nicknames?"

He feigned offense. "I'm trying to find the right one to truly express my undying love."

"Don't you think that's a bit over the top?"

"No more than your Christmas bikini there. Are those matching board shorts?"

I sighed. "Yes."

Josh took one look at my defeated expression and understood. "Don't you think your fiancé should wear them?"

"You don't need to. It was a silly idea even when I had a real boyfriend."

He grinned and took the shorts from me. "I think our love is exactly that kind of silly." Then he disappeared into my bathroom to change and emerged a minute later, sporting the red board shorts covered in lime green Christmas trees. He struck a few model poses until I laughed and threw my hat at him.

"What? I make these look good."

Josh always looked good. His kayaking habit kept him in great shape. At least I was fake engaged to a handsome, humorous guy for the week. I could do worse.

"Come on. You can model those around the pool."

We met Chris in the hallway outside our rooms, and he took one look at our matching swimwear and laughed out loud. "You two have gone over the edge."

Josh slung his arm around my waist and tugged me to him. "No one I'd rather jump off this edge with."

Because no one else would ask him to jump off this particular edge.

Chris shook his head at us and led the way up to the pool deck. Or what he thought was the way up to the pool deck. He swore he had seen a shortcut on the ship map in his room, but we took a wrong turn somewhere, and we ended up winding all the way to the front of the ship and into the art gallery above the theater.

None of us minded the accidental detour. We lingered for a few minutes to appreciate the work hanging in the gallery. The pieces on display were a beautiful mix of abstract landscapes and detailed watercolors and even pencil sketches. There was something for everyone's taste.

I paused to admire an ocean scene done in oil. The rich, deep blues of the water faded into the lighter hue of the sky. The motion of the painting was as calming as its colors.

"That's gorgeous," Josh said.

"It's so tranquil. I feel like I could stare at it all day."

"You know, you could stare at the actual ocean if we find the pool deck," Chris said.

"I'm not the one who found the art gallery instead of the pool," I jabbed back at him playfully.

"Everybody's a critic," Chris said as he led us out of the gallery and found a staircase that looked like it might lead up to the pool.

"Your work could be in there," Josh said to me.

"I don't think so," I said.

"He's right," Chris chimed in. "Your paintings are awesome. I love that one you gave me when I graduated. Me summiting a mountaintop with the whole world below me. It still hangs in my office. It inspires me to new heights every day."

"You are so cheesy," I said.

"Totally serious."

"Hey, do I get a painting now that we're engaged?" Josh asked.

"Don't press your luck," I told him.

"You never painted anything for Josh?" Chris asked.

"No. I only paint for family." Or the guy I'd thought would be family. I should never have painted for Shayne.

My brother clapped Josh on the shoulder. "I'm sure now that you've been elevated to fiancé, you'll get one of Katie's coveted works."

I shook my head. "He'll put it up in the coffee shop."

"Because your work deserves an audience," Josh said. "Would it be that bad to have your paintings adored by my customers? I bet one of those trendy business guys that comes in every morning would pay top dollar for your stuff."

"It's not for sale. That's not why I paint."

"Then don't sell it, but let people enjoy it. It's all I'm saying," Josh argued back.

"Keep saying it. I'm still not listening." I quickened my pace up the stairs.

When we finally found the pool deck, the rest of the family had already staked out a table and a couple of lounge chairs in the shade. Dad and Jacob were absorbed in a friendly game of chess, and Mom said she was perfectly content to read in the shade, but I convinced Amy to move to loungers in the sun with me while Chris and Josh splashed around in the pool.

To avoid any more uncomfortable questions about me and Josh, I started asking Amy about the baby. She happily launched into the plans they'd made for turning one of their spare rooms into a nursery. They had already gotten started painting it yellow and orange and picked out all the new furniture. She glanced lovingly over to Jacob when she talked about watching him put together the crib last weekend. I hoped someday I would share that kind of love with someone. Albeit, someone a little less know-it-all than Jacob.

As I closed my eyes to daydream about when I would meet the guy of my dreams, Josh plopped down on the end of my lounge chair and sprinkled my legs with pool water.

I squealed. "That's so cold."

"Refreshing," he corrected. "Know what time it is?"

"No. Why? Do you have important places to be?"

"Maybe." A mischievous grin crossed his face.

I dug for his phone in my beach bag and handed it to him.

He glanced at the time and the notifications on his screen.

"Anything wrong?" I asked.

"Um, coffee shop emergency," he said. "I'll catch up with you later."

He wrapped his towel around his shoulders and wandered off with a goodbye nod to Amy and me.

"He's up to something," I said.

"What do you mean?" Amy asked.

"Just a feeling." I'd known Josh forever. He wasn't the kind of guy to let work pull him away from vacation. He could have taken a quick call from the coffee shop poolside. Something else was going on.

"Maybe it's a Christmas surprise," Amy suggested gleefully.

I grimaced. The last couple of days, I'd had my fill of unexpected. I did not need any more surprises this week.

~ 10 ~

To Us

THE NEXT DAY Josh and Chris and I relaxed with midmorning coffee on our joint balcony and watched the ship pull into port in Philipsburg, St. Maarten. The rolling hills of the island rose up higher than I expected, and the water in the harbor was the deepest blue I had ever seen. I'd spent plenty of time on the beach in Galveston and along the gulf shore growing up, but those waters couldn't compare to the picture-perfect paradise of this Caribbean island. I suddenly understood why Mom might want to spend Christmas sailing around these seas. The view from our balcony was nothing short of stunning.

The ship docked alongside a long pier that led straight into the heart of Philipsburg, and all the eager tourists poured out onto the pier for their day on the island. We were in no hurry to get off the ship. We had two full days in port, and Mom had scheduled us for a rum tasting excursion for the afternoon, so we had plenty of time to sit back and take in the scenery this morning.

Thankfully, Chris wasn't interested in asking questions about the wedding that Josh and I weren't actually planning, so we talked idly about our ideas for exploring St. Maarten and listened to Chris's funny stories about traveling for work. He always met the most unexpected and interesting people, and my brother knew how to tell a story. One of my favorite things about catching up with him was hearing about his latest escapades. He kept us entertained while we ordered burgers and salad from room service for lunch. Before we knew it, it was time to meet up with the rest of the family.

On my way through my room, I grabbed a sun hat and sandals and checked my green sundress in the mirror as I ran a brush through my loose waves. I looked like any other merry holiday cruiser, not one who felt guilty about bringing a fake fiancé to her family vacation. Maybe no one would bring that up today.

The whole family was waiting for me in the hallway outside our rooms. Their expectant gazes switched from Josh to me, and a new wave of guilt washed over me. So much for putting that to the side today. I tucked my hand into Josh's and said we were ready.

Mom talked excitedly as she led us off the ship and toward our waiting tour bus at the end of the pier.

She told us about their morning learning to fold origami Christmas flowers and how fun the rum tour was supposed to be. Dad added that he'd read all the online reviews, and they promised we would not be disappointed in our excursion choice for the day. Jacob gave us a brief history of the development of rum in the islands.

"Molasses is a byproduct of refining sugar," he explained. "Which the plantation slaves discovered could be fermented into alcohol."

"How interesting, Jacob," Mom said. Then she apologized again to Amy that she wouldn't be able to partake in the spirits.

Chris leaned over and whispered to me, "I feel sorry for her too. She probably needs a drink the most."

I stifled a giggle in Josh's shoulder, and he asked what was so funny. I promised to tell him later.

"I don't mind at all." Amy patted the slight bump in her belly. "I'll just soak up all the Christmas spirit."

She should have no problem with that. An enormous Christmas tree stood next to the Welcome to St. Maarten sign at the end of the pier, and the entire town beyond looked completely decked out for the holiday. Even our waiting tour van was wrapped in garland and sported plastic reindeer antlers above the doors.

Our driver greeted us warmly, and we boarded the van with one other family from Oklahoma, a couple about Mom and Dad's age and their twin daughters who were fresh out of college. They were all very nice and excited to visit St. Maarten for the first time. I was excited that the spotlight seemed to have shifted off of Josh and me for the day. As everyone else talked about how much fun they were having on the cruise so far, I relaxed back in the seat with Josh and watched the bustle of the city pass by on the way to the rum distillery.

When the tour van pulled to a stop, I thought we might be in the wrong place. We'd stopped in a residential neighborhood in front of a giant warehouse. I wondered exactly what kind of tour Mom had booked for us, but the driver cheerily pointed us toward the entrance and told us to have a great time.

An older guy in shorts and a "Rum Today, Rum Tomorrow" t-shirt met us at the entrance and welcomed us to the home of the Caribbean's best rum. He led us inside the immaculately clean warehouse lined with festively colored cases of rum. While he showed us through the facility, he cracked a few bad rum jokes, and we couldn't help but laugh at them. The spark in his eyes showed how much he loved this place, and that was infectious. It was the way I felt about Austin. I'd lived in New York with Chris for a year after college, while I was training to be a yoga instructor, but it never felt like home the way Austin did.

Our guide told us the story of how the distillery got its start in the owner's kitchen as a hobby and grew from there into the international rum business we saw before us today. We got to see how the brightly colored bottles were filled and packaged. Then he led us to the tasting area, tables and chairs made of old rum casks, where we could sample their famous rums or some of their more experimental varieties.

I had expected a few sips of unpalatable hard liquor, but they had a ton of flavors. We all opted for different ones so we could share. We took turns passing around the different flavors. Jacob gave us a couple of unsolicited facts he'd heard on a podcast about rum production. Chris made eye contact with me, and I couldn't help but burst out laughing. Luckily, no one really noticed since they were all busy comparing flavors and deciding which they liked best. My favorite was the raspberry white chocolate. Josh liked the jalapeño lime, and Chris went for the peanut butter cup. Dad and Mom agreed that the cinnamon was the best, and Jacob went for the classic coconut rum. Amy sipped her sparkling water and sniffed each flavor, saying they smelled delicious. I felt sorry for her not being able to enjoy the flavors with us, but she practically glowed with happiness. Being together as a family is what mattered to her.

We should definitely let her pick our restaurant for dinner, though. Then as if the bartender knew I was thinking about food, he brought out rum cakes to sample. I'd thought the rum was indulgent, but the cake surpassed it. It was so moist and delicious.

"These are amazing," I said.

"Maybe you guys should have rum cake for your wedding," Chris suggested.

"Who's getting married?" the bartender asked as he laid another tray of samples on our table.

"My sister here just got engaged to this lucky guy," Chris said, pointing to me and Josh.

"We need a toast to the happy couple then." The bartender lined up another row of taster cups for everyone in the tasting room and filled them with wedding cake flavored rum.

I tried to protest, but he said, "No worries. It's on the house."

Chris and Jacob helped him pass them out, and when everyone had a cup, the bartender raised his glass and said, "May these two find the joy in every sunrise, the calm in every sunset, and the passion in every moon tide. To love and laughter and happily ever after."

"To the bride and groom," everyone echoed and toasted us.

I didn't know what to do. Accepting that heartfelt toast felt wrong. There was no happily ever after to be had here.

Josh tapped his plastic cup on mine. "To us."

That I could drink to. Our friendship was the one thing keeping me afloat on this cruise. "To us."

~ 11 ~

ICING ON MY FACE

AFTER WE'D DRUNK our fill of rum samples and Dad bought us all matching rum pun t-shirts that said "Rum More Time" from the gift shop, we headed back outside and into the gorgeous St. Maarten afternoon. Our driver was leaning casually against the van, waiting to help us back in for the ride to the ship. As we climbed into our seats, he asked if we'd had a good time and suggested other places on the island we might want to see during our stay.

"Why don't we head to the beach for a snack," Amy suggested. "I'd love to stick my toes in the sand and get a little nosh."

I seconded that. It was edging into evening. We'd managed to close down the rum factory tasting room, and I could use something in my stomach other than rum and rum cake. My lunch salad was too many hours past. The guys said it sounded good to them too. No one wanted to end the day so early.

Mom bowed out though. She gave my dad a loving pat on the arm and said she would prefer a quiet evening with him back on the ship. They were #lifegoals personified. Eventually, I would find a love that lasted like theirs.

"Since you're my last ride of the day, I can drop you off at the best beach bar on the island after I return to the pier," our driver offered.

That sounded easier than flagging a cab down, so we rode to the pier where Mom and Dad bid us farewell for the night, and we said goodbye to the family that had been on the tour with us. Then the driver took us over to the Sunrise Beach Bar on Kim Sha Beach. Chris slipped him a nice tip in his parting handshake, and the driver gave Chris his number in case we needed a ride later.

The bar itself looked like every beach bar in the world—thatched roof, wooden stools, and a planked floor that led straight into the sand—but the view from this bar was without equal. The aquamarine waters glinted brilliantly under the sun and beckoned us in. A dozen sailboats dotted the bay, and the sea stretched out beyond them to touch the white puffs of clouds in the deep blue sky.

We took stools at a table facing the water and marveled at the beauty of it until the bartender, a slender woman with weathered skin and a Santa hat cocked on her beaded braids, appeared with cocktail napkins.

"You thirsty folks look in need of some Guavaberry Sunrises," she said.

"Four please," Jacob said, "and non-alcoholic for my wife."

"Drinking for two, eh?" The bartender winked at Amy. "I've got just the thing. Coming right up."

She returned in a flash with four Guavaberry Sunrises, which, true to their names, rose in color from dark orange to light yellow in the glass.

"And one Guavaberry Colada, hold the rum," she said as she sat a Pepto-pink slushy in front of Amy. "You all here for the Christmas party tonight?"

We shrugged, and Chris answered, "Didn't know about a party. We were passing through for a drink and a view."

"Well, you might want to stick around. Band starts in an hour. Bonfire and dance floor on the sand. And, of course, Santa hats for all." She pulled five paper Santa hats from her back pocket and laid them on the table.

"How could we resist that?" Josh said.

"That's what I thought you'd say. I'm Selma if you need anything." With that, she moseyed on to the next table of arriving customers.

"To unexpected Christmas cheer." Josh raised his glass.

We toasted and sipped our drinks. The Sunrises tasted spicy and bittersweet, exactly the way I imagined a tropical Christmas would taste. Amy let us try hers. It was smoother than ours, more like a berry milkshake made with coconut cream.

Josh reached for a Santa hat to place on my head, and soon we were all wearing them and taking beach selfies. When Selma came back to check on us, we took her advice and ordered codfish fritters and Johnnycakes to munch on. Then with so much Christmas cheer in the air, our conversation turned to our favorite Christmas memories.

"I know the perfect one." Chris shot an amused smile in my direction.

"Oh, no. Do not tell that one," I said.

Josh leaned in, curious. "Do tell that one."

"I'm sure you've heard it," I said. I had purposefully never told him this story, and I'd managed to get to almost thirty without my brother telling it to him.

"I'll be the judge of that," Josh said. "And besides, even if I have, Jacob probably hasn't."

Chris took that as his cue to plunge onward. "Katie must have been about four, I think, when Amy and I decided it would be the funniest thing in the world to play a Christmas trick on our darling little sister."

"Oh my gosh, I love this story." Amy clapped her hands together.

Now Jacob leaned in too. There was no turning back.

I groaned.

Chris continued, "She believed in Santa already, but we convinced her that Krampus was real too. Amy and I had seen some show on TV about Christmas traditions around the world, and we were fascinated by this demon-goat figure that punished kids instead of giving them presents. So inspired by that, we told Katie that if Santa Claus left any cookies behind on the plate we set out that it would draw Krampus to the house. Even a leftover crumb would be enough for him to pick up the scent. And for every crumb he found, he would steal a present from under the tree because it meant Santa was dissatisfied with the cookie offering that the kids in the house had provided."

"Oh no," Josh said with a grin. He knew exactly where this was going because he knew the kind of tricks my brother and sister liked to play on me and how gullible I'd been as a kid.

"Oh yes." Chris laughed.

Amy took that as her cue to take over the story. "We stayed up all night watching Kate stay up all night watching to make sure Santa ate every last bite of cookie. Of course, Mom and Dad then stayed up all night waiting for all of us to go to bed so they could put the presents under the tree. Kate finally fell asleep by the tree at some ridiculous hour, like four in the morning, so Chris and I went to bed thinking we'd had our fun."

"But then," Chris interjected, "Mom and Dad put all the presents under the tree, and instead of risking waking her up, they covered Kate up in the chair with a blanket. They took a bite or two of the stack of sugar cookies we'd left on the plate for Santa and went back to bed, knowing that we would all be up way too early to unwrap everything."

"So," Amy picked back up, "while we were all sleeping, Kate woke up again and saw that Santa has obviously been there because the floor around the tree was filled with presents, but Santa had hardly touched the cookies. Afraid that Krampus would show up and start taking presents, she took that plate and sat down on the floor and ate every last cookie."

Laughing hard now, Chris managed to say, "When we got up, she was licking the plate, and she had icing all over her face. All over her pajamas. All over the carpet."

Amy started to giggle. "Our parents were so mad. Since we'd made those cookies specifically for Santa, we'd made every color of icing we could, and it was everywhere."

"Mom and Dad were horrified," I added. "That might be one of my very first memories—their faces staring at me in total disbelief."

Josh chuckled, but he laid a gentle hand on my back. "That's why you don't eat sugar cookies?"

I buried my head in my hands to hide my mortification and nodded. "I'm going to get another round."

"I'll help," Jacob volunteered and hopped off his stool to follow me to the bar.

I ordered another round from Selma, who was hustling behind the bar now that it had gotten more crowded.

"It's not that bad," Jacob said as he leaned onto the bar next to me to wait for our drinks.

He had no idea what it was like growing up with those two. My expression must have said as much because he then added, "Okay, it might be, but I feel for you. I'm the youngest of five."

I'd forgotten that.

"My older brothers convinced me once that dog food was cheese and got me to start snacking out of the dog bowl until my mom caught on."

"That is evil," I said. Maybe Jacob did understand me.

He shook his head. "That's siblings for you."

"Tell me about it. You seem to have turned out fine though."

"Only on the outside." He genuinely smiled then, something I'd seldom seen him do around us. "I'm a neurotic mess on the inside."

"I never would have guessed."

"Really?" he sounded surprised. "I've always been nervous around you guys. Amy has the perfect family. Doting mom and dad. Insanely successful brother. Free-spirited and fun-loving little sister. I didn't know quite where I would fit in to all that, but you guys are so accepting. This trip is making me feel like part of the family."

That made me feel bad for every time Chris and I had laughed at Jacob's expense. The poor guy had been spouting random trivia to us for two years in an effort to fit in. He was trying to be the smart one or something. I never imagined that Dr. Jacob Jones could be as insecure as I was.

"To tell you the truth," I confessed. "I've always felt like a bit of an outsider myself. It's hard to be the youngest when you have to follow in Amy and Chris's footsteps."

Jacob's face screwed up in confusion. "But you don't follow their footsteps at all. You forge your own path out there. It's what Amy admires most about you."

"She does?"

"Yeah, she says she wishes she had your passion. You follow your heart wherever it takes you. She said she hopes our baby will get Auntie Katie's confidence and courage."

That literally left me speechless as we carried our drinks back to the table. I'd spent so much time worrying about how I measured up to my sister that I'd never stopped to think of her doing the reverse or finding anything in me worth measuring herself against. It made me want to be the version of myself that she saw.

When we got back to the table, Josh had changed the subject from my childhood cookie traumas to his favorite Christmas cookie memories. "Mom always saves the sugar cookie baking until Christmas Eve night. We sit around the kitchen, drinking cocoa, and rolling out and decorating cookies. Kate's been there."

"Yeah, it's fun," I admitted. "They still leave a plate out for Santa, and I still somehow end up with icing all over my face."

~ 12 ~

SUNSET AND SANTA HATS

TRUE TO SELMA'S promises, as the sun spread its orange rays across the sky and the first stars appeared on the dark violet horizon, the band began to play and one of the waiters lit the bonfire on the beach. They also turned on the strings of Edison lights strung from the bar to two tall poles in the sand, marking out the dance floor.

"Want to dance?" Josh asked.

"Definitely," I said.

We kicked off our sandals and stepped off the deck into the sand. Neither of us had ever been a good dancer, but that had never stopped us. We'd taken a swing class together in college, and we'd learned some basic steps that we used since for every kind of music. We always got the steps a little wrong, but that never mattered. If anything, it made it more fun.

The band kept it lively with a Christmas calypso vibe and some occasional Latin beats thrown in. Before long, we were laughing our way around the sand together with a dozen other couples in paper Santa hats. Some had wrapped themselves with garland or wore t-shirts printed with ugly sweater patterns. Amy and Jacob joined the crowd, and Chris found a few dance partners to twirl around the floor. The table next to ours had been taken by a group of twenty-something women vacationing together for the holiday. They were more than happy to keep Chris on the dance floor as long as he wanted.

When the band slowed the tempo, some dancers took a break, but Josh pulled me closer. We hadn't slow danced in years, probably since his second cousin's wedding when he'd needed a last-minute date. He'd gone with me to Amy's wedding last summer because it'd been too early in my relationship with Shayne to invite him to a family wedding. But I'd been busy with bridesmaid duties and didn't get to dance much. Tonight, though, we fell easily into the sway of the leisurely beat. Dancing under the stars in Josh's familiar arms with the warm sand between my toes made it easy to forget that we were pretending to be a couple. I had to remind myself not to get caught up in the moment. This was my best friend. We weren't actually dating.

"Should we start making our breakup plans?" I asked.

Josh looked appalled. "That's what you want to talk about while we dance on this beautiful beach?"

"I want to be prepared."

"I don't think being prepared to break up is going to make us look convincingly in love for the rest of the week."

He had a fair point. We already knew this was fake. If we concentrated on breaking up, it would be that much harder to play out the deception that we were planning a life together.

"Fine. What should we concentrate on?" I asked.

He spun me out and back to him. "How about enjoying the week?"

I considered for a minute. "You know what would help me enjoy the week?"

"What's that?"

"Knowing where you went after the pool yesterday."

"Can a man have no secrets?"

So my suspicions weren't unfounded. He was up to something. "Sure. Some other man can."

He sighed. "A jealous wife already."

I smacked his shoulder. "Be serious."

"I told you it was the coffee shop."

"I'm well aware of what you told me. I've also known you long enough to know that's not true."

"Katie—"

"Don't Katie me. I cannot handle anything else this week. If you need to go home or something just tell me."

He stopped dancing and stepped back to look straight at me. "I swear to you it's nothing serious. I wouldn't leave you this week. And I am doing nothing untoward."

I narrowed my eyes. "I'm trusting you."

"You can always trust me." He bowed low like a courtly gentleman making a noble promise. Then he took my hand and twirled me around again.

Back in his arms, I leaned quietly into him and wondered what he would feel the need to hide. My sister was probably right. Josh was likely concocting some fun Christmas surprise, but I couldn't imagine what. He shouldn't be doing anything. Coming on this vacation with me and pretending to be my fiancé was present enough. I would be hard-pressed to find something that extraordinary for him when I got the chance to shop. For now, though, I let it all go. I breathed in Josh's familiar scent mixed with the warm ocean breeze and took his advice and enjoyed the moment.

As full darkness set in, the flames of the bonfire beyond the dance floor crackled and soared up into the sky full of twinkling stars. The waves lapped at the shore, and the excited voices and laughter of the revelers mixed with the steel drum of the band, adding merry accents to the festive music. I glanced over at our table and saw Chris's eyes wander our way while he talked to Jacob and Amy.

"I have one more serious question," I said.

"Spill it, Honey Bun."

"Yesterday with the high five—"

"Yeah, sorry." He cringed. "I forgot we were engaged for a minute there. I tried to cover it with a kiss on the hand. I think that worked."

"Yeah, super smooth, but I thought we should set some ground rules for our public displays of affection. So we can keep it in mind for the rest of the week."

"Sure. Ground rules. I like a woman who knows what she wants. What did you have in mind?"

"I'm not sure."

He laughed. "Or not."

I was suddenly nervous talking to Josh about this. I was never nervous around Josh. That was the beauty of our friendship. Maybe I was pushing that friendship to its limits this week. I had to be careful not to push it so far that it broke.

"Well, what says we're engaged without crossing a line?" he asked.

"I like the hand holding. That's totally convincing."

He nodded.

"And obviously arms around each other more. You know, standing closer than we normally would."

He tightened his arms around me. "That I can do."

I rested my chin on his shoulder and tried to ignore the fluttering in my belly. I'd never felt like this being close to Josh. Something was different tonight. Something had changed. I tried to ignore it and continue the conversation. "The forehead kisses are good. That feels intimate."

"And the cheek." His soft voice tickled my ear and sent a pleasant shiver down my spine.

That had definitely never happened with Josh before.

"Yes, but not the lips. That would be too weird." I leaned back to clear my head from the dizzying attraction I was feeling in his arms, but he was holding me so close, that put us face to face.

Our lips were almost touching when he whispered, "Yeah, too weird."

We froze like that for a long, tantalizing moment. I'd never wanted so much to close the short distance between us and feel Josh's kiss. My heart thumped in my chest as he closed his eyes. My breath hitched in my throat as I closed mine and waited.

But instead of the brush of his lips or the soft tickle of his stubble on my cheek, I felt his forehead rest gently against mine. A shred of the catastrophic heartbreak that would come from being romantically rejected by Josh tore at my heart. I couldn't afford to confuse our pretend romance with a real one. He meant far too much to me. Losing him would be a devastating wound that would never heal.

I wrapped my arms around his neck and held on tight for the rest of the song.

~ 13 ~

SET MY HEART STRAIGHT

I SLEPT LATE the next morning. Josh, Chris, and I
hadn't quite stayed to see sunrise at the Sunrise Beach
Bar, but I don't think we'd missed it by much. Amy
and Jacob had been the sensible ones and caught a
cab around midnight. After the near-disastrous kiss
on the dance floor, I'd made sure that Josh and I
stuck to quick tempo songs only and hung out with
Chris and the new friends he'd made. Along with his
dance partners at the next table, we'd met a lively
mix of tourists and locals who had definitely been in
the mood to celebrate Christmas in the tropics. They
bought so many rounds of rum shots, I eventually
started tossing them over my shoulder and sticking to
water. I knew my limits, and I hadn't wanted a buzz
pushing me past my heartbreak boundaries with
Josh. I'd successfully avoided doing anything I
couldn't take back.

When the sun beamed full strength through the
sliver in the curtains onto my pillows, I finally

hopped out of bed, stretched, and slowly moved through my usual yoga practice. I was in no hurry today. No one had set any agenda for us. Mom had told us all to spend the day in St. Maarten however we wanted and meet back on the ship for dinner after sail away. I showered and dressed in shorts and my new purple Rum More Time t-shirt. Then I pulled my curtain back to see if Chris and Josh were out on the balcony soaking up the last of the morning sun.

Josh was alone, leaning on the railing and squinting pensively across the island. He'd put on his rum shirt too and a pair of cargo shorts. We'd look like twin tourists today. Except where my shirt was baggy, his tall, muscular frame filled out his tee. I bit my lip with the realization that I wasn't objectively admiring Josh's strong physique. I found him enticingly attractive.

I was now attracted to my best friend! This was so not good. *What am I doing?* I thunked my head against the door.

Josh started at the noise and turned around with a questioning look.

I slid the door open and poked my head out. I skipped right over any explanation of why I had felt the need to bang my forehead against the glass. "Hey, you're up."

"Yeah. Chris left with Amy and Jacob earlier. I think we're the last ones out today."

"Oh." *Great.* We were going to spend the day alone together. Two days ago, I would have been overjoyed at that proposition. Now I needed time away from our pretend engagement to get my feelings back in check. I could not be attracted to my best friend. He had always been an incredibly handsome guy, and that had never stirred these feelings in me before. My heart was simply very confused by my recent breakup and how close our fake relationship had brought us in the last couple of days.

"I wanted to check out Front Street," he went on. "The one the driver told us about yesterday. I need to get in some last-minute Christmas shopping. We left in such a hurry, I don't have any presents for your family."

"You don't have to do that."

He grinned. "I want to be the best son-in-law-to-be that I can. I've started to ask myself 'what would Jacob do?'"

"Go overboard to please people apparently," I said, remembering my conversation with Jacob last night.

Josh shrugged. "It's working for him so far."

WE MADE OUR way off the ship and down the pier. Josh had already talked to the Excursions Concierge before I woke up, and he found out that we could walk along the tourist boardwalk over to the shops on Front Street without taking a cab.

The sunshine and fresh air warmed my skin and rejuvenated my spirit. Walking side by side, but not hand in hand, I felt like we'd returned to our usual selves. No one was with us to be pretend engaged for. I changed my mind about the day. This was exactly what I needed—time alone with Josh my best friend instead of Josh my pretend fiancé. That would set my heart straight.

It turned out the boardwalk on the way to the shopping district was also full of shops, so we wandered into t-shirt and souvenir stores as we went. We tried on silly hats and laughed at the sayings printed on funny t-shirts. We pondered who would buy some of the more obscure souvenirs and sampled some local candies.

By the time we reached the cobblestone streets and the colorful colonial buildings lining Front Street, we were more than ready for lunch. I hadn't even had breakfast. We found a cafe where we could sit outside under the palm trees with a view of the bay. We snacked on conch and dumplings and tried some famous St. Maarten spare ribs. Being from Texas, we were always skeptical of "famous" barbecue anywhere else, but those ribs were fall-off-the-bone tender and glazed with a sweet, spicy sauce. We ate every bite.

Josh leaned back in his chair and patted his belly. "That was awesome. I need more days like this in my life."

"Stuffing yourself with ribs?" I asked. "You know we can do that in Austin."

"True." He sipped his beer and looked out over the calm waters of the bay. "But this is the perfect day in paradise with perfect company."

I couldn't argue with that. I'd thought I wanted to be here with Shayne, but being here with Josh was better. I wasn't trying to be good enough for anyone else when I was with Josh. I could just be me. That's what best friends were for. Maybe that's all we would ever have if we couldn't find our respective Mr. and Mrs. Rights.

"Josh, whatever happened to Lisa?" She'd been the last girl he'd dated, a PhD candidate in biomedical engineering at the university, but that had been more than two years ago now, and he'd never really told me what went wrong between them.

His expression saddened. "Are you intent on not enjoying this with me?"

"Come on," I prodded. "Maybe if we understand what keeps going wrong in our love lives, we'll eventually learn how to make it go right. Then we can share days like this with our significant others too."

He crossed his arms on the table and leaned toward me. "I don't know if you heard, but my love life is looking up. I recently got engaged without even knowing about it."

I gave him a wry smile. "She left for Chicago, and you hardly said a word about it."

"Fine." He threw his hands up in defeat. "I'll tell you what happened. I hesitated."

"What does that mean?"

Josh stared down at the remains of the ribs on the table. "I think she was expecting a ring for graduation, and I gave her concert tickets."

I gasped. "You never told me that."

"I never told anyone that. I knew something had to change when she graduated, but I wasn't sure what, so I didn't do anything. I never even talked to her about it. Whatever it was between us, I let it slip away. She accepted that job in Chicago, and that was that."

I thought back to that summer. I'd been dating a musician and spending a lot of time at his shows down on Sixth Street instead of hanging out with Josh. I should have been there more for Josh, but by the end of the summer, we'd both been single again and had more than enough time for each other. "Wait, is that why you had VIP Ed Sheeran tickets?"

"Yep."

"I can't believe she gave them back."

He rubbed his hands over his face like he could wash away the memory. "She'd left town by then. She wasn't going to fly back for it."

Just when I thought I knew everything about my best friend, I learned something new. My heart ached for him, but he hated sympathy. He wasn't one to wallow in sorrow, which is probably why he'd never told me the details of their breakup in the first place. So instead of hugging him and telling him it would all turn out okay in the end, I tried to make light of it. "Her loss. That concert was amazing. I'd take it over a ring any day."

That made him laugh. "And that is why I choose you, my little Guavaberry."

I laid my hand over his on the table. "You know, I think when you find the right girl, you won't hesitate at all."

He squeezed my fingers in his. "I think you're right."

Contentment spread over my heart as I met his sweet brown eyes. I counted myself lucky to have such a friend. Life would be less without him. This week was certainly making that clear.

The waiter interrupted the moment with our check, and I let go of Josh's hand to reach for my wallet. I tried to pay for lunch since he was going to buy presents for my whole family, but he wouldn't let me. He knew I didn't have an extravagant budget, so he rarely let me pick up the check. I thanked him, and we left our beachside table for more shopping. We hadn't actually bought anything yet, and Josh insisted that he needed something for everyone on the trip with us.

We ducked into a chocolate shop first and tasted our way through their samples for our dessert. Josh got assorted truffles for my mom and sister, and I bought a box of them for an emergency late-night room snack.

"I might sneak over in the middle of the night for those," Josh said.

"I'll be sure to lock my balcony door," I teased.

At the rum shop, he picked up a bottle of everyone's favorite flavor from our tasting yesterday. Then we headed into a jewelry shop because he thought my mom and sister might like something shiny.

"Well, I've never known them to say no to jewelry," I said.

We looked over their selection of bracelets and earrings to find the best ones. I helped Josh pick out a pair of sapphire earrings for my mom and a tanzanite bracelet for my sister. They would love those and adore that they were from Josh. Well, until we fake broke up.

Of course, as soon as I thought about our fake engagement, we stumbled upon the ring counter. I let myself gaze for a moment at the rings sparkling under the display lights. The blue diamonds caught my eye. The way they twinkled reminded me of the sun on the sea. Some day, someone would love me enough to want to give me one of those.

"Can I show you any of our engagement rings?" The saleswoman asked as she finished wrapping Josh's purchases.

"Oh, no." I quickly backed away from the counter. "Just admiring."

"Which one would you want?" Josh surveyed the shining diamonds as if he were seriously considering picking one out right then.

I tugged at his arm to pull him away from the counter. "I could never pick. I'd want to be surprised."

He didn't budge. "That does make it more fun."

"What kind of ring would you buy?" I asked tentatively, holding onto his arm and peeking back at the display.

With an endearing grin, he said, "I'll know the perfect ring for the perfect girl."

~ 14 ~

TROPICAL SNOW

AFTER THE JEWELRY shop, we split up for a little while to shop on our own. Josh wanted to pick up a couple souvenirs for his family, and I still needed to get him a Christmas present. I'd originally intended to find a gift for him on this trip since I wouldn't have seen him till New Years, but now the pressure was really on to get him something awesome. I had no idea what would be good enough to say thanks for coming on this trip last minute over the holiday and pretending to be my fiancé all week. I wandered in and out of the shops aimlessly picking things up and putting them back down. Nothing seemed quite right. Josh wasn't the kind of guy that put much stock in material things anyway. A seashell clock or a bottle of sand would just collect dust on his shelf. Frustrated and tired, I took a break on one of the wooden benches on the sidewalk.

While I sat there sipping coconut water and racking my brain for good ideas, I saw Josh slip back into the jewelry store. He must have decided to get that emerald necklace he'd been eyeing for his mom when we were in there. He was too sweet. He deserved the best of everything. If I had his knack for picking out great presents, I'd have found him the perfect thing already.

Ultimately, I gave up trying to find the right thing and bought him a bottle of rum and a giant box of truffles. At least I knew he'd like those. I planned to add a homemade coupon redeemable for a free fake fiancée anytime he needed one. That would make him laugh.

I met him back at the restaurant where we'd started, and we took our time strolling toward the ship along the shore. We tucked our flip flops into our shopping bags and walked where the waves could lap over our feet. We weren't the only cruisers spending the last few hours in St. Maarten on the beach, but it was far from crowded. It was the right amount of busy to make you happy that other people appreciated the sunshine and the sand as much as you did.

It reminded me of our walks along the lake trail at home. At least once a week, Josh would pick me up from the yoga studio with iced lattes from his coffee shop, and we'd set out for an evening walk together. We never cared that we'd traced those steps a thousand times before. We just wanted good company to watch the sunset over the lake. It was one of my favorite things about living in Austin. One of the things that made it feel like home.

"It doesn't get any better than this," I said as I tilted my head back to soak in the sun.

"Actually, I've got something you might like better."

"Really?" That piqued my curiosity more than a little.

But all he would say was, "You have to see this for yourself."

We made our way back onto the ship and stored our packages in our rooms. Josh insisted that I change into long pants, which I argued was an odd request, but I obliged and threw on some yoga pants. He'd changed into jeans and his Keep Austin Weird zip hoodie. Way overdressed for the tropical weather outside, he led me downstairs into the lower parts of the ship that I hadn't explored. The corridors in the lower levels seemed narrower and darker since only small porthole windows offered a glimpse of the tropical sun outside.

"Where are you taking me? I feel like you're the phantom of the opera luring me into the depths of the opera house."

"Muhahaha," he gave his best evil laugh. "I can't teach you how to sing though. So don't expect that."

"Oh, I would never. I've heard your out-of-tune karaoke. But where are we going?"

In answer, he led me through a lobby and up to a set of double doors marked "Cherish Rink."

"Rink?" I barely had time for that to set in as he pushed through the doors and escorted me into a dark, chilly room. In front of us was an honest to goodness ice skating rink.

My jaw fell open.

"I know it's not snow, but it's the best I could do."

He'd managed to find me a hint of a wintry Christmas in the tropics. I grabbed his face between my hands and planted an appreciative smooch on his lips. "You are amazing."

He smiled broadly. "Finally, my talents are recognized."

Only then did I realize I'd broken our fake engagement rule of no kissing on the lips, but he hadn't seemed to mind, and I hadn't felt any weirdness about it like I had last night. This was just the two of us being us. No silly rules needed.

We slipped into skates and made our way out onto the ice with a few other couples who had also decided ice skating on the ship was preferable to the beach. A multi-colored disco ball spun circles of light around the ice, and early 2000s pop music played over the sound system. If I'd still had braces, this would be exactly the same as the last time we'd been skating. Except Josh wasn't a lanky teenager anymore. He offered me a strong, steady hand as I wobbled onto the ice, unsure of the blades on my feet.

I reached for the padded wall, but he tugged me gently away from it.

"You got this." He offered up his other hand and skated backward in front of me, pulling me forward.

I'd forgotten about his hockey phase. During sophomore year, he'd thought he was destined to be the next Wayne Gretzky for at least a semester. Then he'd discovered kayaking, a much more reasonable sport for Texas, and he'd never looked back. I was thankful for the hockey blip though as he coaxed me around the rink. He was much more at home on the ice than I was.

A couple of rounds in, he let go of my hands, and I drifted slowly by myself.

"Don't go too far," I pleaded.

"I'm right here." He skated to my side and rested a reassuring hand on the small of my back.

I pushed lightly off one blade and then the other until I was skating under my own power. I was probably going turtle slow, but it was fast enough to pick up a cool breeze from the ice and chill my cheeks. I giggled at the wonderful absurdity of the moment—ice skating on a ship in the middle of the Caribbean. It was better than Rockefeller Center.

We lost all track of the hour as we circled the ice together. It wasn't until the rink started to clear out that we realized it was nearly dinnertime. We rushed out of our skates and dashed upstairs so we wouldn't be late, but that left us totally underdressed. Josh had wrapped me up in his hoodie when I'd gotten cold on the ice, so I was in yoga pants and an oversized tie-dyed sweatshirt. Josh was still in his jeans and rum t-shirt, but the hostess didn't blink an eye. She simply greeted us with her usual cheer and led us to our table.

Chris was the only one seated. Everyone must have had a good day in St. Maarten if they were running late too. He took one look at our pink cheeks and our casual clothes and laughed. "Good day?"

I beamed at Josh as he pulled out my chair for me. "The best."

~ 15 ~

A Sweet for My Sweet

THE NEXT DAY we all wandered in to breakfast at a leisurely pace since we were at sea all day with nothing planned. My sister waited until everyone was seated to announce that she had arranged a special treat for the whole family that day, inspired by Josh. That prompted a flood of questions and guesses about what she had planned for us, but all she would tell us was to dress for a mess and meet at ten o'clock sharp at the Italian restaurant. When I said that I didn't think they were open that early, she smiled coyly and said we'd see. What was with everyone and their surprises this week?

Josh knocked on my door at a quarter till. He was still in the same jeans and t-shirt he'd worn to breakfast. His casual style was always prepared to get messy, a necessity for running a coffee shop. I'd changed out of my sundress and into shorts and a tank top and pulled my hair into a ponytail. I was prepared as I could be for my sister's mystery experience.

"What do you think she has planned?" I asked as I slipped into the hallway with him and pulled my door shut.

"Must be awesome if I inspired it," Josh said.

I slapped his arm playfully, and he took the opportunity to take my hand. That was starting to feel like second nature—my hand in his. I'd miss that when we got back to our real lives next week.

At the Italian restaurant, a beautiful brunette woman named Tori checked off our names as part of the Greyson family party and showed us in. Like the dining room, this restaurant was lined with windows overlooking the magnificent Caribbean ocean view. Each table was stacked with bowls, sugar, flour, cookie cutters, and everything else we'd need to make sugar cookies.

"Of course." I sighed in resignation as the need for Amy's subterfuge set in.

Josh laughed and threw his arm around my shoulders. "Your favorite, Sugar Bear."

Amy waved us over to a table by the windows.

"The things I do for love," I whined.

Once the whole family had gathered around our table, our waiter introduced himself while he filled our cups with eggnog. He pointed to the laminated cookie recipe at the center of our table and explained that we were free to make as many cookies as we wanted. As we filled each baking tray, he would whisk them off to the kitchen for baking and return them cooled for decorating.

"How delightful," Mom exclaimed. "Amy, this is wonderful."

Dad picked up a snowman cookie cutter and said with some amusement in his voice, "And I see why it was a surprise."

"I couldn't get her here any other way," Amy said.

"It's all for Josh," I said.

He hugged me close and gave me a kiss on the head. "You're the best present a guy could get."

I squeezed my arms around his waist and hoped he meant that. Otherwise he might be disappointed in his bottle of rum and fake fiancée coupon.

"Your family does bake the best cookies," Mom said. "Someday I'll have to get your mother's recipe."

"I might be able to sneak it out of the kitchen for you." Josh gave Mom a conspiratorial wink.

Jacob got us all organized, and Amy started measuring out flour and sugar. Josh volunteered to stir, and I volunteered to watch while I sipped my eggnog. Pretty soon, we had an assembly line set up. Josh convinced me to help him mix up the dough. Amy rolled it out. Chris and Jacob cut the cookies out, and when they came back freshly baked from the kitchen, Mom and Dad iced them. They also dotted each other's cheeks with icing like they were newlyweds cutting their cake together. Someday I would find a lasting love like that.

Within a couple of hours, we were all covered in flour and icing and looking at a couple dozen festive sugar cookies. We'd been having so much fun baking together that no one had mentioned careers or accomplishments. For the first time in a long time, I hadn't felt measured against my siblings or pressured to be more than I was. Instead of feeling inferior, I felt like part of the family.

Josh dabbed my nose with a floured finger and handed me a heart-shaped cookie decorated with red and green icing and sprinkles. "A sweet for my sweet."

"When did you make that?" I asked, touched by his thoughtfulness.

"When you and Amy were deciding if all the reindeer needed red noses or not."

A classic Christmas debate. She was on the side that there should only be one Rudolph, and I thought they all deserved red noses. Ultimately we compromised and gave the snowmen red noses, which Chris then objected to because snowmen were supposed to have noses made of coal.

"Are you going to eat a sugar cookie?" Chris asked with a raised brow when he saw the cookie in my hands.

The whole family turned to pay attention to that. I hadn't eaten a sugar cookie since the infamous Krampus debacle.

"Nope, but I will cherish it forever." I carefully cradled the heart cookie to my chest and gave Josh my best adoring smile.

"You two are too cute," Amy said.

Only for a couple more days. Then we'd be just friends again. That thought made me sadder than I wanted it to. I really liked it that Josh had baked me a special heart-shaped cookie. He was playing his part too well, and my feelings for him were getting muddled again now that we were back together with the family and in full-on fake engagement mode. This week was a rollercoaster of emotions that couldn't end soon enough.

Our waiter boxed up our cookies so that we could take them back to our rooms, and we all decided to clean up and catch a buffet lunch. Josh excused himself, saying he had some business to tend to, making sure the coffee shop was set to close up for the holiday tomorrow. But he promised to meet up for dinner and the tree trimming party in the evening.

"I wouldn't miss that for the world," he said. "We have to see if Kate's gingerbread shipbuilding talents won us first prize."

~ 16 ~

BROTHERLY ADVICE

EVERYONE HAD SOMETHING they wanted to do for the afternoon. Amy was excited about the skating rink that Josh and I had told her about last night, so she and Jacob went to take a few laps around the ice. Mom took Dad to check out the sales at the onboard shops for last-minute stocking stuffers, and Josh disappeared for "work," although I was sure that was code for finishing up his mysterious Christmas surprise. I managed to suppress my curiosity enough not to follow him and see where he went, but I was still dying to know what he was up to. A surprise from Josh could be anything from a homemade cookie, like I'd gotten this morning, to a Happy Birthday written in the sky, like he'd done for Lisa before they broke up. I hoped it was more on the cookie end of the spectrum. He'd already gone far beyond what any friend should be expected to do this week.

Left to ourselves, Chris and I decided to head up to the Sundeck Bar and enjoy the beautiful weather from the top deck. A low-key afternoon with my brother sounded like the perfect chance to unwind from this whirlwind week. We rarely got to hang out in person anymore. We'd resorted to video chats lately, but that wasn't the same as the long Saturday afternoons we used to spend on the rooftop of his building in New York drinking cheap beer and talking life, dreams, and everything else. We found an empty table by the railing under the shade of an umbrella and ordered the drink of the day, Candy Cane Cocktails, from a handsome bartender named Marty.

"I talked to Jacob the other night," I said as Marty left to prepare our drinks.

"I did see Mr. Useless Knowledge corner you at the beach bar. Let me guess, he told you how many tons of sand were on the shore? Or more about the origins of rum production on the islands?"

"Actually, he told me more about his family, and I think we've been too hard on him."

Chris raised a skeptical brow. "Really? Does he come from a family of trivia champions, and that's the only way they communicate?"

"Chris, I'm serious."

"Okay, okay, my peacekeeping little sister. What's his sad story?"

I didn't want to repeat his dog food story. Chris would find that too funny. Better to only give him the gist. "He's trying to fit in. He wants to find his place in the family."

"With little known facts he picked up on podcasts?"

I shrugged. "I didn't say he was good at it, but I get where he's coming from. He's doing his best to get us to like him. Let's give him a break, and try being nice to him."

"I am nice to him."

I pointed an accusatory finger at Chris. "No more eye-rolling."

Chris grimaced. "You drive a hard bargain. What do I get out of this deal?"

"My respect."

"I already have that."

I gave him a disapproving frown. "You're too self-assured. How about a better relationship with your brother-in-law?"

He threw his hands up in surrender. "Fine."

"Pinky swear."

He held out his hand and locked pinkies with me. "I will do my best to make Jacob feel more welcome," he promised. "I'll take him mini golfing or something tomorrow."

"Thank you. Was that so hard?"

He chuckled as the bartender returned with our drinks—martini glasses filled with a slushy red and white liquid swirl and rims coated with crushed candy canes.

The first sip was like a peppermint explosion in my mouth. "Wow, this tastes like Christmas."

"Not a bad way to spend the holiday," Chris said, taking a drink of his own.

We sat quietly for a few minutes, soaking in the scenery—nothing but blue waves as far as the eye could see. The mellow pool band music drifted over the top decks, and the other cruisers around us seemed as carefree as we were, sipping Christmas cocktails on the deck of the gently rolling cruise ship. Christmas at sea was winning me over. We could make this a holiday tradition.

"I've never seen you this happy," Chris said.

I took in a long slow breath of ocean air. "This is pretty amazing."

"I mean with Josh."

"Right." For a moment there, I'd let myself forget about the mess of deception I'd created this week.

"I have to admit I almost thought you were joking at dinner the first night. I couldn't believe you hadn't told me when you guys got on the ship, and I was asking about Shayne. You know that was the perfect opportunity to say, 'yeah, well, I've got somebody much better than him. I'm engaged to Josh now.'"

"That would have made sense." If only Chris had said so that first night, maybe I would have taken that way out and told everyone we were joking instead of letting it go this far.

He swirled his drink around his glass. "But I guess I get it. You wanted to tell everybody together and get the whole family reaction at one time."

"Yeah, of course." I had to wait for everyone to be sitting around the same table talking about their awesome life accomplishments before I felt totally pressured into making up this insane engagement story.

"It's big news, and I already told Josh this, but if I could pick somebody for you, it'd be him, Katie. Nobody makes you smile like Josh does. He brings out the best in you."

I shifted uncomfortably on my chair. I wanted to tell Chris the truth. We'd always been close, and he was obviously a little hurt that I hadn't told him first about the engagement. If it'd been a real engagement, Chris would have been my first call with the exciting news. Now it was doubly awkward that I couldn't tell him that Josh wasn't really going to be his new brother-in-law. "Chris, what if he's not the one?"

Chris's expression scrunched up in disbelief. "Wait. Are you second-guessing this?"

"I, um..." I had no idea how to finish that sentence without confessing the whole story, and I wasn't sure I was ready for that, no matter how guilty I felt keeping it from Chris. Part of me didn't want to let go of the idea of being Josh's fiancée, even if it was all pretend. I needed my big brother's advice on how to get out of this, but I couldn't figure out a way to ask such a convoluted question.

He sat his drink to the side and leaned forward on the table. "Look, I can't tell you what to do, and I've never even come close to asking a girl to marry me, but I can tell you that when I do, it will be because I feel about her the way Josh feels about you."

Maybe Chris could answer my question without me having to ask it outright. "What do you mean? How do you know how Josh feels?"

"Because he told me. You are what matters most in the world to him."

That didn't clear anything up. Was that Josh acting as my fake fiancé, or Josh starting to get confused about his feelings while acting as my fake fiancé? Sorting the pretend feelings from the real ones was getting way too complicated. And obviously, I was horrible at judging these things. I'd completely misread my last boyfriend's intentions. That's what had gotten me to this point in the first place. I had to end this soon before one of us got our heart broken.

"He means the world to me too," I said. Because no matter what else was going on, that was the truth.

~ 17 ~

TRIMMING THE TREE

WE MET BACK up with the rest of the family for dinner, and they chatted excitedly about their afternoons. I listened to Mom's shopping stories and Amy's ice skating adventure as I sipped on my sparkling water. I didn't have anything to add. I didn't want to relive my talk with Chris with the rest of the family. When he recounted our afternoon to them, he only mentioned the tasty cocktails and the limitless ocean view. He did make a point to ask Jacob how he liked the ice skating, which I appreciated. At least I'd done some good this week.

I tried to follow the family conversation as it bounced from one story to another without letting my eyes wander too often to Josh. He'd changed into dark jeans and a starched white button-up with a black striped tie. Those were his "date" clothes. He only changed out of his trusty t-shirts when he was bent on wooing a girl or impressing her family. I knew it was all an act this week, but Chris had planted a doubt about that in my head. And with that came a secret hope that I hardly wanted to admit to myself. Deep down, there was a part of me that wished this relationship was real, and that sent my thoughts into a tormented spin. I couldn't let myself fall for Josh because I couldn't risk losing him.

As we left the table after dinner, Josh pulled me aside. "Are you okay? You were a million miles away at dinner."

"Yeah." I rubbed my tense neck. Apparently I hadn't succeeded in hiding my disconcerted mood as well as I'd wanted to. "I think I'm just tired, you know."

He laid a comforting hand on my shoulder. "It's been a long, strange week. We can head back to the balcony to relax after the tree trimming, watch the ocean go by under the stars. Then we'll be rested up for the big Christmas Eve Ball tomorrow."

I nodded. An evening watching the slow rhythm of the waves from our balcony did sound stress relieving, but I did not share his enthusiasm for the ball—another event where our fake engagement would be on full display. I longed for another day alone with him, where we could go back to being just us, like we'd had shopping and ice skating yesterday. Unfortunately, for the rest of the cruise, that wasn't possible. We were stuck on the ship for the next two days at sea with the entire family and the lie we'd told them.

Josh lifted my chin up, so I had no choice but to meet his reassuring gaze. "Let's go get some Christmas cheer at the tree trimming. It'll make you feel better."

On any other occasion, he would have been right. I loved Christmas parties. I was usually all about everything holiday. I adored the twinkling lights and jolly spirit that this time of year brought with it. But tonight, I wavered when I looked into Josh's eyes. I'd made a mess of this, and it might already be too late to turn back. Trimming a tree with our fellow passengers was not going to change that.

"We'll make this the best Christmas ever." His eyes twinkled like he knew something I didn't.

That sent an unsettling tingle down my spine. I hoped he knew what he was doing because I wasn't sure of anything anymore. I let him take my hand and pull me along after the family for the ship's official tree trimming party.

As we entered the atrium, we were greeted by a string quartet playing Christmas melodies. Elaborate candelabras and the giant Christmas tree reflected in the tall windows. Waiters carried trays of champagne and baskets of ornaments. Everyone had a chance to choose an ornament and have their picture taken with Captain Karlsson as they hung it on the tree. Josh picked a miniature painting of Santa and Mrs. Claus on a beach for our ornament.

"That's ridiculous," I said.

"Definitely not as good as your paintings, but kind of sums up our week, right?"

If he meant a fantasy relationship on a beach, he was totally right.

We hung our contribution on the tree, and I gave a half-hearted smile for the camera. Then I excused myself to the ladies' room. I wanted to put some distance between Josh and me. Being near him was too confusing. I was way too drawn to him tonight. I needed time to myself to think through how we were going to get out of this week without permanent emotional scars.

On my way out of the atrium, I ran into the girls from the family who had been on the rum factory tour with us. They complimented the floral handkerchief dress I'd thrown on for dinner, and I decided talking to them would be distraction enough to settle myself. Thankfully, Josh joined Chris across the room in a conversation with a couple of other guys. I turned my back to them and listened to one of the girls talk about picking the right grad school for architecture. I told her about the university in Austin, and I felt the tension easing in my body as I answered her questions about my hometown.

When I glanced over my shoulder to check that Josh was still across the room, I saw him standing next to a lithe redhead. She threw her head back in laughter at something he said, and an unexpected wave of jealously rumbled through me. It occurred to me then that she might be the reason he'd been sneaking off this week. Maybe it wasn't some Christmas surprise that he was planning at all. Maybe he had found someone to fall in love with on this cruise ship like we'd joked about on day one, and I had been a complete fool to think he might be getting confused about his feelings for me as I was obviously doing for him.

I wanted to slap myself on the forehead. I had no right to feel jealous. I shouldn't feel anything but happy for my best friend—as he'd always been for me.

"I need some fresh air," I said to excuse myself from the conversation.

I made my way toward the sliding doors to the outside deck. But the cruise director's voice stopped me in my tracks. She'd taken the mic and thanked us all for coming. I reluctantly turned around. I had to stay for the awards presentation, in case my ludicrous gingerbread ship actually won something.

"And now, the moment you all have been waiting for," she said. "The votes have been tallied, and it's time to announce the gingerbread decorating winners, who will each take home one of our fabulous Cherish Cruises trophies." She held up the stylized pink cruise ship again for us all to admire.

Dad gave me a thumbs up from across the room, and Mom smiled brightly at his side.

Nicole announced third place, and it wasn't us. Then she announced second place, and again, it was not us. Each of those families accepted their trophy and got a winner's photo in front of the Christmas tree with the captain.

I nervously glanced in Josh's direction. The redhead had moved on. He caught my eye and gave me a confident wink. Even if we did win, it wouldn't stop the anxiety roiling in my belly.

"And first place," Nicole said, "for their imaginative gingerbread cruise ship goes to the Greyson family."

The crowd clapped and cheered as my family made their way to the tree for the trophy presentation and picture. It took me a minute to convince my legs to move that way. I might not have made it at all if it weren't for Amy tugging on my arm and leading me toward the rest of the family as she and Jacob made their way forward.

Nicole presented the trophy to Mom and Dad, but Mom insisted that I hold it front and center for the photo since it had been my idea that won us the contest. Josh slid his arms around my waist as the whole family squeezed together in front of the tree and congratulated me on my award-winning creativity.

Pride should have been swelling in my chest. This is what I'd wanted—to be appreciated by my family for my talents. But the whole ceremony swirled around me like an unreal daydream. The lie I'd told to get to this moment overshadowed all of it. Josh's embrace felt false, and the encouragement from my family felt unearned. Only the hard plastic of the trophy digging into my overly tight grip felt real.

After the camera stopped flashing, I tried to hand the trophy to Mom. I imagined she and Dad would take it home to set out on the mantle each Christmas as a reminder of our vacation together, but she pushed it back into my hands.

"Oh, no sweetie. You should take it home with you and Josh. It can be your first decoration for your new home together."

I didn't know what to say to that. There would be no new apartment with Josh. The corners of the smile I had managed to plaster on my face slipped down. I stared at the trophy so I didn't have to meet anyone's eyes.

~ 18 ~

ONE MORE DAY

ON CHRISTMAS EVE, I rose early enough to greet the sunrise over the ocean. The first pink tendrils of light pushed into the purple twilight as I unrolled my yoga mat on the balcony and moved through my Sun Salutations in the calming ocean breeze.

I'd turned down Josh's invitation to lounge on the balcony after the tree trimming party last night and gone straight to bed instead. That had given me the time I needed to step back and seriously rethink the situation. I'd woken up with new clarity this morning. I didn't have to let this spiral any further out of control. I didn't have to let the guilt sit like a heavy stone in my belly like it had after my talk with Chris yesterday. I didn't need to let jealousy cloud my judgment about my true feelings of friendship for Josh. And it was friendship I felt for him. It couldn't be anything more. The simple, if painful way out of this, was to come clean to the entire family, and I would do it today. I stood in Mountain Pose with my eyes closed and my hands at my heart and tried to ground myself, but it was hard to get in touch with the earth in the middle of the rocking sea.

"Morning, Sunshine." Josh's voice startled me, and I almost fell over.

I righted myself with the help of the railing and turned to find him already fully dressed, back in his casual cargos and t-shirt, with two steaming coffee cups in his hands. This was the Josh I was used to. Things were going to go back to normal today.

"Latte?" He handed me one of the cups.

"Thank you." I sipped the coffee and savored the heat of the cup in my hands and the warmth of the drink in my empty stomach. "What are you up to? I didn't even hear your door open."

He glanced over his shoulder to the curtain-covered balcony door. "I was trying not to wake Chris. We stayed up pretty late talking after you went to bed. Did you sleep well? Feel better this morning?"

"Much," I said. The best I had felt all week. I finally had a plan and the courage to follow it.

"You seemed pretty deep in thought out here. I almost snuck back inside. I didn't want to interrupt, but I wanted to make sure you were okay. You weren't yourself last night."

"I'm not sure I've been myself at all this week." I tapped my fingers on my cup. "I'm glad you came out though. I wanted to talk to you this morning. I was thinking about this whole thing between us."

He stepped closer. "I've been thinking about it too."

"You have?"

"Of course. I can hardly think about anything else."

Had it been torturing him too? He was so easygoing, sometimes it was hard to tell when things really bothered him. But if it had been consuming his thoughts as much as it had mine, then he'd be relieved with my resolution to tell the family the truth today. "I'm going to tell them today."

Confusion wrinkled his brows like he didn't know what I was talking about, like somehow he'd forgotten about our whole fake engagement. Maybe it was too early in the morning. He'd had a short night. I needed to be clearer with what I was saying.

"I let this go on for too long. I should have stopped it before it got this far. I should have never put you in this situation in the first place. I'm going to make it right today."

His face creased with worry instead of the relief I had expected. He sat our cups down on the table and took my hands in his like he had something very serious to say. "Do me a favor, Katie, please. Don't do it today."

"What? Why not? Don't you want to get this over with?"

He'd been the one who wanted to tell the truth from the start. He'd been right about that all along. I should never have let him backtrack on that just because everyone had gotten excited about the two of us together.

"I don't want to..." His honest brown eyes searched mine, and I knew I'd do anything he asked me to today. "I don't want you to miss the ball tonight."

Was that his concern? He'd done so much for me this week. Being my date for the ball would be one more thing to add to the long list of things he'd done to make me happy.

"It's okay," I tried to reason, even though I was enticed by the idea of going to the Christmas festivities without my family being furious at me for lying to them all week. I couldn't be selfish in this any longer. I'd been too self-absorbed lately. It was time for that to stop.

"I want to take you to the ball," he said sincerely.

"You do?"

"I do." He pulled my fingers to his lips for a chivalrous kiss on the knuckles. "It would make me the happiest man on this ship."

He always knew how to get me to smile. No wonder I'd thought I was falling for him. Josh was impossible not to love. My earlier resolve melted. One more day wouldn't matter that much in the whole scheme of things. Right? That rock of guilt could settle into my belly until tomorrow, and I could spend one more day separating my pretend love for

Josh from my friend love for Josh. I'd done it for almost a week already. Not entirely successfully, but I could try again. For him.

I pushed playfully at his chest. "Fine, I will permit you to take me to the ball, Prince Charming."

Relief washed over his face, and he flashed me his sweetest grin. "Great. Now I just need a fairy godmother to wave her wand for my tux."

~ 19 ~

SOAK IT ALL IN

AFTER BREAKFAST, THE guys whisked Josh away to see to his tuxedo rental since he'd packed in such a hurry he hadn't had time to think about bringing something formal for the ball. Not that he owned something that formal in the first place. There were some nice suits hiding in the back of his closet, but those rarely saw the light of day. I didn't think I'd seen him in a tux since college, but he seemed more than game for it today. He happily wandered off with Chris and Jacob and Dad for a guys' day.

Mom had arranged for a separate girls' day— pampering at the spa. I wasn't about to object to that. Relaxing at the spa would give me time to make a plan for confessing everything to the family tomorrow, not to mention making my skin a little more radiant for the ball tonight.

The spa was as jaw-dropping as the rest of the ship. Travertine tile, soft light, and marble statues of Roman gods filled the space. We started with the

Roman bath experience, soaking in a warm pool and then a hot tub. Luckily, they were designated quiet spaces, so we couldn't talk about the things I didn't want to discuss anyway. It was exactly the peace I needed.

When I'd soaked long enough to turn my fingers pruny, I reclined on one of the heated tile loungers overlooking the ocean in the aptly named Reflection Room and breathed in deeply. I rehearsed in my head how I would confess to the family in the morning. I'd tell them I'd gotten carried away and beg their forgiveness for Josh's sake. At the very least, I could salvage my friendship with him. And that's what mattered most. My family's opinion of me would lower, but they'd never held me in that high regard in the first place. They'd chalk this whole fake engagement up to another amusing story that Chris would get a kick out of telling at cocktail parties. Embarrassing as that would be, I'd learn to live with it. Eventually.

By lunch, I was satisfied with my plan and ready to do the right thing, as soon as we got through the ball. For the time being, I joined Mom and Amy for made-to-order salads in the spa dining room. We sat on remarkably comfortable contoured stone benches as we listened to the soothing sounds of a trickling water feature and piped in orchestral music. We talked about Mom's volunteer work with the Junior League and Amy's ER work. They asked about the different yoga classes I was teaching at the studio, and Amy asked if I could show her some good prenatal stretches. I talked her through a few right then and promised to show her more back in our rooms.

After lunch, we started getting ready for the ball with manicures, pedicures, and blowouts. I never treated myself to this kind of luxury in Austin, so I pushed all worries aside and let myself enjoy every moment of it. I hadn't hung out with my mom and sister like this in years, and without Josh by my side, the pressure of the fake engagement lessened so much, it almost disappeared.

Until, of course, the conversation inevitably returned to my impending fake marriage. As we settled into the massage chairs for our pedicures, Mom said, "I know you and Josh got engaged very recently, but have you thought about wedding plans at all?"

I did not want to talk about planning a wedding that was never going to happen. I needed to find a graceful way out of the conversation without making my mom and sister feel like I'd shut them down completely. We'd been having such a lovely day together. I didn't want to ruin it with more lies when I was on the verge of telling them the truth.

"Not really," I answered. "It was all so sudden. I think we're going to take our time and really think things through before we make any plans."

"Of course. You two have all the time in the world," Mom said as she handed her wine-colored polish to the attendant.

I handed the attendant the light pink color I'd selected and breathed a sigh of relief. Maybe saying that we wanted to take our time would be enough to get away from the uncomfortable topic.

"Yes," Amy chimed in. "You should explore all your options to make sure you love your wedding day as much as you love Josh."

"Right." I took a long slow sip of champagne. As much as I loved Josh. That was the big problem I'd never seen coming this week. My feelings for him had gotten way too confused when he pretended to love me. He played the part of doting fiancé too convincingly. I needed to keep my attraction to him in check today so there would be no awkwardness between us when we went back to normal tomorrow.

"Are you guys thinking Austin?" Amy asked. "Or a vacation destination? You could do a cruise! If I could do mine again, that's the only thing I might change. It was a perfect day in Dallas when Jacob and I got married, but there's something romantic about being on this boat. Maybe it's seeing you two in love." She droned on dreamily, so unlike her usual matter-of-fact ways. Pregnancy must bring out her fanciful side.

"Um, we are having a great time on this trip. Everything has been so fun, don't you think?" I asked in a lame attempt to change the subject.

"It really has," Mom agreed. "My favorite part is seeing all of my kids happy."

That was a good segue. We could talk about how happy she was for Chris and Amy. The irony was not lost on me that for the first time in my life, I'd really gotten Mom's attention, and the only thing I wanted to do was steer her thoughts right back toward my siblings. I was deciding whether Amy's pregnancy or Chris's move to Manhattan would be more distracting, when Mom said, "I know that Josh has the means to give you the wedding of your dreams, but your father and I want to help. We helped Amy and Jacob, and we want to do the same for you."

"Oh, thank you," I said because there was no other response to that other than the obvious *I'm not really engaged!* that I wanted to scream out. But I'd promised Josh that I would make it through the ball without confessing our secret. For whatever reason, he wanted to go without upsetting the status quo today. Maybe Chris had told him something in their talk last night that made him think we needed to wait another day. I should have asked more questions before they ran off for the guys' day. Or run off with them. They were probably playing mini golf on the upper deck while I was getting the third degree about our non-existent wedding planning.

"It's the least we can do, sweetie." Mom reached over to squeeze my hand in hers, and I swear her eyes were moist with tears.

I swallowed hard and managed to give her a weak smile in return. I was going to break everyone's heart when I told them the truth. Maybe that's what Josh had learned from Chris last night.

"Have you decided when you'll have kids?" Amy asked.

Panic constricted my throat, so all I could manage to do was squeak out a quiet, "What?"

She patted her belly. "Well, if it's soon, our kids will be nearly the same age. Wouldn't that be adorable?"

I'd chastised myself for wanting to kiss Josh earlier in the week. My mind certainly hadn't wandered to having kids with him.

"Amy," Mom said. "Give her time to soak this all in. They have plenty of time for children."

I downed the rest of my drink and asked the attendant for more. This was going to be a long afternoon.

~ 20 ~

NEW MOVES

ALONE IN MY room, I put the finishing touches on my makeup and gave myself a pep talk in the mirror. I had survived the afternoon thanks to some deep breathing techniques and a spa attendant who was liberal with the champagne pours, but the whole experience had rattled me almost as much as lying to Chris's face yesterday. Being fake engaged was harder than I'd imagined and for more reasons than one.

"We are almost there," I said to my reflection as I applied my rose pink lipstick. After tonight, we could tell the family the truth. Although, I'd spent the afternoon waffling between telling everyone tomorrow like I'd planned or waiting till we got home so the family could enjoy Christmas day without any of my personal life drama. As guilty as I felt listening to Mom and Amy make wedding and married life plans for me, they were so delighted doing it. I was no longer sure I could abruptly end all that tomorrow. I might be the unsuccessful daughter, but I didn't also want to be the daughter who ruined our family Christmas cruise. I'd talk it over with Josh when we got a moment alone tonight. He would help me make the right choice. He'd helped me get this far.

In the meantime, we could try to enjoy the Christmas Eve Ball. I'd bought this dress specifically for the occasion when I'd thought Shayne was coming with me. I'd imagined the floral sequins on the mesh overlay of the long blush maxi shimmering under the starlight as we danced in the open air atop the cruise ship. But Shayne was a couple thousand miles away with someone else in his arms, and it was raining here. I ran my hands through my loose curls and straightened my posture. None of that would stop me from having a fun night with my best friend.

Amy and I opened our doors at the same time to meet in the hallway. Her blonde curls bounced over her shoulders, and her a-line little black dress swung playfully above her knee. She was radiant, from her candy red lips to her matching heels.

"I'm famished. You think they'll have food at this thing?" she asked.

"Has there been a moment on this cruise that didn't include food?" I answered.

"Good point."

She knocked on Mom's door. Mom took a minute to come out, but Dad would say she was well worth the wait. She wore a classic floor-length wine gown with a three-quarter-sleeve sequin bodice. Her sleek bob swept dramatically across her forehead, and her smokey eye makeup highlighted her light eyes. All class from head to toe.

The three of us couldn't look more different, but Josh had told me once that differences made family stronger. After spending the full day with my mom and sister at the spa, I thought he might be right. Maybe like Jacob, I was starting to find my place with this family. Only I was about to ruin that by telling them I'd deceived them all week. I bit my lip and decided that was a point in favor of waiting until after Christmas to tell them I was not engaged to Josh.

We made our way to the dining room, which had been transformed for the ball. The regular dining tables had been cleared from both levels. The entire bottom floor was now one huge wooden dance floor ringed with bar tables. Upstairs was the ultimate Christmas lounge with dozens of cozy groups of couches and chairs set around coffee tables, like an upscale hotel lobby decorated for Christmas. A good crowd was already lounging back with hors d'oeuvres and cocktails. A mix of flickering faux candles and twinkling white lights gave the room a warm glow, and glass icicles and snowflakes cascaded over the dance floor to create an elegant winter wonderland. Several couples were already swaying their way around the floor to the lilting ballroom music.

Dad caught our attention and waved us over to one of the tall tables near the windows at the end of the dance floor, where the guys stood waiting for us. My heart stilled at the sight of Josh—striking in a burgundy tux jacket with a sleek black vest and a classic bow tie. When we got to the table, he leaned in to kiss my cheek. His intoxicating new cologne filled my senses, disorienting me for a second. His smooth jaw brushed mine, and I realized he'd shaved. Almost as long as I'd known him, Josh had had a perpetual two-day stubble, but tonight, he was clean-shaven, and his usually slightly disheveled hair had been mussed perfectly to beckon a girl to run her hands through it. He was every bit the tall, handsome fiancé that I would have dreamed of having at my side. I tried to recover my senses as I stepped back. I had to keep our real relationship clear in my mind.

His gaze swept down my dress. "You look ravishing."

That hardly helped me think straight. I'd never heard Josh utter those words about anyone, let alone me. I couldn't suppress a smile at the compliment. "Thank you."

Chris and Josh volunteered to get drinks for us and headed to the bar.

Amy nudged me with her elbow. "Josh looks pretty good tonight."

Watching him walk away, I had to agree, but I also had to take a deep breath and tell my excited heart to settle down. Even devastatingly suave Josh in a tux was still Josh my best friend. I could not forget that.

"We'll have to toast you two again when they get back with our drinks," Mom said.

"No. That's all right." I tried to wave her off. "We've had enough toasts this week."

"Oh, don't be modest," Amy said. "You have to celebrate the good things. Aren't you the one who told me that?"

"I probably got that from an inspirational calendar," I said.

She laughed. "No, you didn't. You got that from one of your yoga seminars. That retreat you went to in Sedona."

"You remember that?" I didn't think my sister actually listened to anything I said.

"Of course. You are always full of sage advice. That's how I describe you to everyone. My little sister, the guru."

That surprised me and warmed my heart. My sister kept proving my assumptions about her wrong this week. We really should talk more often—if she wanted to talk to me at all after I told her the truth about Josh and me.

Chris and Josh returned with their hands full of drinks and asked how we had liked the spa. When we told them how relaxing it had been, all of the guys vowed they would spend part of Christmas day there tomorrow. Their day had apparently been a more random adventure that included a hole-in-one mini golf tournament they'd stumbled upon in the afternoon. Dad turned out to be a mini golfing ace, unbeknownst to all of us, and had sunk more holes-in-one than anyone else on the ship, which won him one of the coveted Cherish Cruises trophies. We all congratulated him on his win.

"Even at my age, you discover some hidden talents," he said as he proudly straightened his bow tie.

I sipped the sweet champagne Josh had brought me and reveled in the family banter as the guys tried to convince Dad to join the mini golf pro circuit.

"There is no such thing," Mom objected.

"Actually, there is," Jacob chimed in and enlightened us all. "The US masters have been held for over twenty years, and European tournaments date back to the 1930s."

"You're kidding?" I said.

"Not at all."

Of course he wasn't. Jacob would know.

Chris clapped him on the back. "What would we do without you, man?"

Jacob beamed.

Having that talk with Chris about being nicer to Jacob may have been the only thing I did right this week. At least I could feel good about that when this was all over.

"This is such a wintry paradise," Amy said as she glanced around the room. "I'm starting to think you two really should get married on a cruise ship so we have an excuse to do this again."

"That's not a bad idea," Chris said. "When do you guys think you'll tie the knot?"

"I, uh, we're not sure," I said, taken aback by the sudden turn of the conversation.

"Kate." Josh stepped toward the dance floor and extended his hand. "I believe they are playing our song."

I gladly took his hand and let him whisk me away to the other side of the room, far from the uncomfortable questions about us. Instead of taking my hands for our go-to swing steps, he pulled me close with a firm hand at my waist and clasped his other over mine at our shoulders.

"What's this?" I asked.

"A little Christmas surprise for you, Buttercup."

Josh led me through some basic ballroom dancing steps without once stepping on my toes. He gently pushed my hip or pulled at my shoulder to tell me when to turn, and before long, we were gliding around the floor like pros.

"Who are you? And what have you done with Josh? When did you learn to dance?"

With a pleased gleam in his eyes, he warned me, "Don't get too excited. These are the only steps I know."

"I didn't realize you knew any."

"I took a couple lessons this week. I couldn't go embarrassing my fiancée at the ball." He twirled me out for a turn.

"That's where you've been sneaking off to?"

"Guilty as charged."

"You are too much." That was by far one of the sweetest things anyone had ever done for me. And now I understood why he hadn't wanted me to ruin the day with a confession of our fake engagement. With that kind of news, we probably wouldn't have attended the ball at all, and he wouldn't have gotten to show me his surprise.

The rest of the family joined the dance floor for the next song. I recognized Chris's partner as the redhead I'd spotted talking to Josh at the tree trimming party. I'd done my best to let go of any lingering jealousy over the way he'd made her laugh, but I still wanted to know who she was.

I nodded toward them. "Do you know that girl? The one dancing with Chris?"

Josh spun us around so he could see her. "Yeah, that's Erica, my dance instructor. You've got her to thank for my fancy footwork."

I should never have doubted Josh's intentions for a moment. He hadn't been off, preoccupied with finding the woman of his dreams this week. He'd been off learning how to dance so we could have a great time together tonight. He was absolutely the best.

"I introduced them at the party last night," Josh explained. "Looks like they are hitting it off."

Erica was obviously amused with whatever animated story Chris was telling her. "Seems like it."

Josh and I danced more than we rested that night. We were having so much fun together. I could forget the stress I'd created for us this week. As the hour grew later, more couples crowded the dance floor around us, and Josh pulled me closer to him. I didn't object. I liked being so near him. Every time I'd tried to put distance between us on this trip, he'd told me to let go and enjoy the moment, so I finally decided to take his advice. I laid my head on his shoulder, closed my eyes, and let him lead us slowly around the floor.

The soft hum of the crowd, the calming rhythm of the music, Josh's warm arms around my back—it all entranced me like a beautiful dream that I didn't want to wake up from.

"This is amazing," I whispered to him. "You've been amazing this entire week."

"You bring out the best in me."

I quivered at his soft voice in my ear. He brought out the best in me too. That's what Chris had said.

Josh brushed his lips over my cheek then and sent my world spinning.

Without thinking, I let desire lift my lips to his. I gave in to the urge I'd had since that night on the beach. I needed to know what Josh's kiss felt like. He didn't shy away as he'd done before. He leaned into me and pulled me tighter into his arms. His kiss was tender and slow and filled with all the longing that had been building between us for the last week. Maybe for the last decade. I gave myself into him fully, and it was easily the most passionate kiss of my life.

I pulled back breathless before I wanted it to end because I knew my heart could break into a thousand pieces if I let it love Josh like that. I couldn't lose my dearest friend over this. But when I looked up into his adoring face, I didn't see my best friend anymore. I saw the man that I loved.

I didn't know what to do with that. I slid out of his arms and backed away from him. The pained confusion in his expression was too much to bear. I ran out of the room.

~ 21 ~

WHAT YOU DESERVE

"KATE," JOSH CALLED after me as I ran all the way up the stairs to the aft deck. "Wait."

I couldn't stop. I had to get out of there. I needed open air to breathe, to think. I was panting by the time I reached the top of the ship and darted into the warm rain, but I didn't care. I might have just made the biggest mistake of my life. How could I kiss my best friend like that? I ran to the back railing and wished I could run farther. All the way back to St. Maarten. All the way back to Austin. Somewhere where life made sense.

"Katie," Josh caught up to me and spun me toward him. "Tell me what's wrong."

"I can't do this, Josh. Not with you."

His face was streaked with rain and worry. "What do you mean? Why not? Why not with me?"

"It's too complicated. We can't keep lying. It's so confusing. I don't even know which way is up anymore." I tried to run my hands through my hair, but it was a sticky mess of drenched, hair-sprayed curls.

"Hey, hey," he said softly. He stepped closer and swept a string of wet hair off of my face. "It's okay. It's just me and just you. Right here."

My voice cracked as I tried to explain the storm of emotions rolling through me, "We are the problem. I can't lie about you and me anymore. It feels too real. This whole pretend thing has gotten way out of hand. We've been doing it so well all week. We're caught up in it now. We can't tell what's real and what's fake."

"Come here." He tried to pull me to him, but I pushed back.

"Don't."

His embrace was the opposite of what I needed to clear my head. Being in his arms was what had gotten me all mixed up in the first place.

He let go of me and dropped his hand to the railing. "Then listen to me, please. It's not a lie. Not anymore. It may not have started out that way. We may have been playacting in the beginning to ingratiate you with your parents, but something happened this week. I thought you felt that. That kiss back there. That was real."

I shook my head. "No, it wasn't. None of this is."

"Are you honestly telling me you don't feel something happening between us? That everything this week—all of those moments we've shared have been a lie?"

I hesitated. I'd never seen him this unsure of himself. Of course, I'd felt something this week. We were pretending to be in love, and I'd found myself thinking I was in love with my best friend. I couldn't do that. I couldn't let us continue to be all mixed up. We needed to get back to the way things were. "I haven't done anything honest all week, and neither have you. That's the whole point here."

He threw his hands up in exasperation. "That's not the point at all. That's just an excuse. The point here is that like everything else in your life, you don't believe in yourself enough to think you deserve it."

"Deserve what?" I raised my voice, almost yelling in my frustration. "A fake fiancé? Planning a future that's going to vanish the moment we step off the boat? Because that's what I had to do all day with my mom and sister."

He stilled and stared into my eyes as he almost whispered, "Love, Katie. You deserve love. Unpredictable, unexpected, all-consuming love. The way I love you."

Those words hung in the air between us like an albatross. As much as I wanted to, as much as I thought I felt it, I couldn't say it back. We'd deceived everyone this week, including ourselves. This was no more real than it'd been with Shayne. I'd been mistaken with him. I was mistaken now.

"That's not how life works, Josh. You don't magically turn around one day and realize the love of your life has been standing in front of you for a decade and a half."

"What if it does?" he asked. "What if all those doomed relationships, all of my hesitations with the wrong girls, all of your off-beat, flaky guys, what if none of that worked out because it was all leading to this? Us. Together."

I searched his hopeful eyes. What had I done to us?

"Katie—" He reached for my cheek.

I backed away from him, unsure of everything now, unable to risk our friendship any further. "Stop, Josh, before either of us gets hurt by this."

Too late. A tear trickled down his agonized face. The damage was already done, and I was to blame.

"This is over," I said with as much finality as I could muster while holding back my own tears. "I'll tell everyone in the morning. You shouldn't be there. I'll take all the responsibility for this. I'll make sure they know that none of it is your fault. I'm sorry."

With nothing else I could say, I left him there in the rain and hurried down the stairs, hoping he wouldn't follow. I couldn't do anything but run away as the tears ran down my face. Every staff member I passed on the way to my cabin asked in worried tones if there was anything they could do for me. I must have looked dreadful—drenched and crying. I shrugged off their concern and quickened my pace toward the solitude of my room. I doubted anyone could do anything to fix the mess I'd made of things. As I shut the door behind me, I wondered if I'd closed the door forever on my friendship with Josh. I rested my forehead against the cool metal and let my tears fall to the carpet.

My heart ached like it might split me in two. Josh had been my constant for literally half my life, and I had carelessly thrown that away because I'd been too prideful to admit the truth to my family. Instead of owning up to the fact that I was nowhere near where they expected me to be in life, or even where I wanted to be, I'd taken the low road and made my worst fear come true—losing Josh. I would never recover from that.

I shivered. The air conditioning chilled my wet skin, so I shucked my dress off. It was probably ruined. Like my life. I left it puddled on the floor where it fell. I toweled off and pulled on my favorite elephant-themed sleep cami and shorts. Then I grabbed my box of emergency truffles from the desk and saw our picture tucked into the mirror. The one we'd taken by the Christmas tree at the beginning of the week when we were definitely just friends and Josh had been doing his best to make me laugh.

I snatched the photo and snuggled under the covers with my box of chocolates. My fingers trembled as I traced his smile in the picture. In one week's time, I'd changed that happy-go-lucky grin into the excruciating grief on his face tonight. He'd fallen into the same trap I had, believing what we were feeling was real. He thought he loved me. I'd thought I'd loved him for a minute there too. But that couldn't be true.

I popped a whole truffle in my mouth. Its decadently sweet taste did nothing to improve my mood. Wasn't chocolate supposed to make you happier? I ate another one, in case it was a matter of dosage.

Closing my eyes, I deepened my breathing. One long inhale and one long exhale. One after the other, again. I tried to settle my mind, but Josh's words kept echoing in my head. I deserved to be loved—by him.

That was contrary to everything we'd ever decided about our relationship. I remembered distinctly the one late night our freshman year of college when we'd sworn to be friends forever and nothing else. We'd been hanging out alone in his dorm room watching *The Princess Bride* because my roommate couldn't stop talking about that movie and we'd never seen it. The conversation had inevitably turned to finding true love. We joked about making a marriage pact in case neither of us found someone by the time we were forty, which seemed very far away at eighteen. But we'd very seriously agreed that our friendship was way more important than romantic love, because in all our experience, romantic love flamed out pretty fast. Our friendship lasted through our toughest times though. We were always there for each other, and that had held true for the last ten years. Until now.

I nibbled through nearly half the box of truffles debating whether Josh could be right. Could I be mistaken about being mistaken? My long string of failed relationships made it pretty obvious that I was inept at judging guys' true feelings about me. Maybe I was just as bad at judging my own. Maybe Josh and I had become more than friends this week. But if that were true—and that was still a big if—the really important question was, should we? Could we risk our lifelong friendship on love? That could end in total annihilating heartbreak. I didn't want to imagine life without Josh. But maybe that's why deep down, I wanted the love between us to be real. Was that what he wanted too?

A tap-tap-tap on my balcony door startled me. The room steward had pulled the curtains across the sliding doors at turndown service, so I couldn't see out, but it had to be Josh. Everyone else used the cabin door. And no one else was desperate enough to stand out there in the deluge tonight.

I ignored the sound, thinking he'd go away, but he kept knocking, followed by a muffled "Katie, please."

He had to be soaked to the bone out there. I wanted to let him in and give him a towel and apologize for everything, but I couldn't face him right now. He couldn't fix this. We were way beyond double fudge cookie frappuccino trouble here.

I had to tell the truth to the family in the morning. I owed them that. I needed to clear the air with them and focus on salvaging what was left of their good graces.

Then I could face Josh with a clear conscience and see how we really felt without the pressure of the fake engagement pushing us together.

~ 22 ~

SOMETHING TO TELL YOU

CHRISTMAS MORNING, I laid in bed until the last possible minute. I couldn't even bring myself to do a single Sun Salutation, which had been the way I greeted the day for years. Instead, I quickly showered and threw on the last sundress hanging in my closet, the red one. It was supposed to be a cheery Christmas color, but I'd left all of my Christmas cheer on the beach in St. Maarten. We were hundreds of miles from there now, physically and metaphorically. I wrapped my wet hair into a messy bun and plodded slowly to breakfast. My flip-flops echoed down the long, empty hallway. I hadn't noticed that sound earlier in the week, but I hadn't been alone all week. I'd had Josh by my side. I'd put a hard stop to that last night.

When he'd quit knocking on my balcony, I'd gotten up to peek outside and make sure he wasn't slouched sadly against the door in the rain. I'd been relieved to see he'd gone, but that didn't stop me from spending the rest of the night fretting over the way I'd left him.

I hadn't slept more than a couple of hours. My eyes were so puffy makeup wasn't going to save them, so I hadn't even bothered with it. I must have looked worse than I thought because the dining room hostess toned down her usually chipper greeting and asked if she could get me anything. I told her thanks but no thanks and walked past her to our usual table.

Everyone was already there, except for Josh. His seat was noticeably empty next to mine. The family quieted as I walked up. Mom stopped mid-sentence in whatever she'd been saying to Amy.

Chris stood up and pulled out my chair for me. "Are you okay?" he whispered.

I nodded and wondered how much he knew. Had Josh told him everything last night? He had to have noticed Josh Romeo-ing on the balcony. Was Chris judging me right now for being so inconceivably awful? It didn't matter. I was about to tell the whole family everything. They could all judge me at once.

Nobody else said anything as the waiter filled my coffee, and I refused to look at them until I'd downed some caffeine. I poured some sugar in my cup and took a long drink. Then I met the worried faces of my family. Did they already know? Or did I look that out of sorts?

"I have something to tell you," I said. "This is hard to say, so please let me say it first, and then we can talk about it."

Everyone nodded their assent.

I took a deep breath and exhaled it long and slow, if a bit shakily. I could get through this if I did it quickly before I lost all my nerve. I glanced at Mom, and her sad eyes convinced me to stare at my coffee cup as I spoke.

"Josh and I are not engaged. We were never engaged. I'm sorry I lied to you. I made the whole thing up because I didn't want to look like a failure who can't keep a relationship or get a real job. Josh had no idea I was going to tell you that we were getting married. I didn't even know. The truth is I invited him along this week because he's my best friend in the whole world, and that's the same reason he played along with the deception. He just wanted me to be happy. Please don't blame him for any of this. I asked him not to be here this morning so that I could tell you the truth myself. I've already asked too much of him this week."

The stunned silence stretched on longer than I could stand. I dared to look up and saw Jacob giving me a compassionate nod. Amy gaped at me, disbelieving and unblinking. Mom placed her hand over her heart like I'd wounded her, and Dad's expression was a mix of confusion and disappointment.

Those were exactly the looks I'd wanted to avoid all week. My chin started to wobble. Then hot tears spilled over my cheeks.

Chris scooted his chair closer and laid a comforting arm around my shoulder. He handed me a napkin to wipe my eyes, and as I buried my face in it, I heard some sympathetic murmurings from around the table. Someone said something about "back to the room."

"Come on," Chris said as he stood us both up and took a room key from Dad.

He kept his arm around me and guided me out of the dining room and down the hallways toward our rooms. The world was once again a blurry haze through my tears.

"I'm sorry," I mumbled.

"You really made a mess of things, little sister."

Chris opened the door to Mom and Dad's room and let me in. Their room was twice the size of mine, with a full sitting area and a curtain closing off the bedroom. I collapsed into one of the two armchairs, and Chris brought me a box of tissues.

"I didn't mean to ruin Christmas," I said as I blew my nose.

He knelt next to my chair and rubbed my shoulder. "It's not ruined. Don't be dramatic. It's different than we planned. That's life."

"How can you be looking on the bright side of this already?"

He chuckled. "Well, I am older and wiser. When you get to the ripe old age of thirty-four, you too shall know all."

"Don't make me laugh. I don't deserve it this morning."

He sighed and took a seat in the other armchair. "Yeah, you do."

"You sound like Josh." I crumpled up my tissues and looked around for a trash can.

Chris grabbed the wastebasket from under the desk and sat it by my chair. "Because that's what he'd tell you this morning too, and you know it."

"I don't want to talk about him right now." I couldn't let myself worry about how I'd hurt him in all this because that would break me down fully. The heartbreak on Josh's face was seared into my memory.

"Okay." Chris didn't push. If he'd spent the morning consoling Josh, he could probably guess how close to the edge I was too.

"Well, my older, wiser brother, what do I do now?"

"Take one of those deep breaths you always tell me to take. The rest of the family will be here in a couple minutes. They wanted a place to have a family talk that's not in the middle of a room full of strangers."

I rubbed my temples. "I should have thought of that." It would have saved me the embarrassing public confession at breakfast. All the people who had wished Josh and me well on the first night were probably whispering about my broken heart now and wrongly assuming Josh was the one to blame.

"You weren't thinking straight."

"The understatement of the year." I hadn't been thinking straight since Shayne broke up with me.

A keycard clicked the lock and the door swung open. My heart leapt into my throat. Time to face the family.

~ 23 ~

THE TRUTH OF THE MATTER

I'D STOPPED OPENLY weeping by the time the family filed into the room, but that meant I could clearly see the mix of pity and befuddlement in their faces. Amy patted my arm as Chris gave her the chair next to me. Jacob stood behind her and gave me another supportive nod. He looked like he was at a funeral. A funeral might have been more fun. Chris leaned against the wall and crossed his arms. He kept his eyes on Mom and Dad as they walked in and sat together on the couch across from me. Chris had been the sweet older brother I needed this morning, but I wondered how mad he was that I hadn't told him what was going on this week. I was regretting a lot of things at the moment, and not confiding in him was topping the list. I didn't want him to think I didn't trust him, and I didn't want him to doubt our whole relationship after hearing what I had to say.

"Sweetie." Mom leaned forward with hands braced delicately on her knees. Her diamond snowflake earrings caught the morning light streaming through the balcony door. She was a Hallmark vision of Christmas in her forest green sweater set. A perfection I would never live up to. "We want to understand what you told us. It's okay that you're not engaged to Josh, but why on earth did you tell us you were?"

There it was. The start of the conversation I'd been dreading for pretty much my entire life. I let out a long defeated sigh as I glanced from Amy to Chris. I'd never told them how inferior being compared to them made me feel. It was no fault of their own. They were born to be great. I wasn't. I never blamed them for it. I blamed my parents for holding me against that unachievable standard, but it'd never been something I'd ever felt like admitting. I'd always thought saying it out loud would make me seem like a petulant child. But now I owed them all an explanation for my behavior this week, and that was the honest truth behind my crazy lie. I was constantly telling my yoga students to be true to themselves, as Josh had astutely reminded me earlier in the week. It was beyond time I took my own advice.

"I told you I was engaged to Josh because at dinner that first night, I felt like a second-rate citizen in this family. Amy had given us her great news about the baby, and Chris had given us his great news about his promotion. And once again, like always, I had absolutely nothing to contribute but a broken heart. I thought I would be introducing you all to my future husband this week. I thought Shayne would be the one, but he wasn't. The truth is he broke up with me the night before the cruise. He left me for a younger, perkier version of me."

Chris chuckled. "That's hard to imagine."

Mom shushed him and told me to continue.

"I called Josh, and I was so upset he volunteered to come along for the week as my friend, my best friend. Then when we got here, I took advantage of that friendship. In a moment of panic, I made up the ill-conceived story about being engaged, and amazing friend that Josh was, he went with it and asked questions later.

"We were going to tell you the truth the next morning at breakfast because he had talked sense into me by then, but when I showed up, you guys were so excited that he... we changed our minds and decided a little white lie—okay, a giant whale of a lie—could stand for the week. We would stay fake engaged and have some kind of fake breakup once we got back to dry land and figured a less dramatic way out of it."

"Honey," Dad said. "Why would you feel like a second-rate citizen?"

Of course that's the part he had latched onto.

I cleared my throat and said the thing I'd never brought myself to say out loud to them, "I don't measure up to Chris and Amy."

"Who's doing this measuring?" Dad asked.

I shrugged and avoided my parents' eyes.

Mom leaned back and took his hand. "Isn't it obvious, Frank? We are."

Dad's brow furrowed like he couldn't comprehend that. "That's nonsense," he told her. Then he turned to me. "We would never compare you kids. That's like apples and oranges."

And I'm the apple that fell very far from the orange tree. "I know it's silly."

Amy laid an understanding hand on my arm. "It's not silly at all. I've felt that way forever."

"What?" Dad and I asked at the same time.

"Katie's so passionate," Amy explained. "About her work, her life, everything. Every time I talk to you guys, I hear all about how she's volunteering at the soup kitchen or teaching at a yoga retreat for disadvantaged kids or hanging out with the hippest new band on Sixth Street because she's dating their drummer." She directed her next words to me. "Your life could be a guidebook for how to live every moment to its fullest. Who wouldn't be jealous of that?"

I opened my mouth, but no sound came out. I had no response to that. Amy, my super put-together, terribly smart, highly educated older sister, thought I was leading an admirable life?

"She's right," Chris said. "You're the one who always seems to know how to squeeze the most out of every drop of life."

"For real?" I tried to live my life in the moment, but mostly that resulted in a lot of wonderful moments on a totally teetering foundation.

"You're the one who convinced me to give my all to my work," Chris went on. "Remember when you lived with me in that horrible apartment in Queens while you were yoga instructor training, and I was stuck in middle management? We used to lay on that rooftop and dream about someday. You told me to reach out and grab someday right then. You told me I had to put my all into it, or it wasn't worth doing. So I did. I took my little sister's advice, and now I'm moving up to my dream job and my dream apartment."

I couldn't take credit for that. "That was all your hard work."

He waved off the compliment. "I mean, how hard is traveling around, taking people for drinks, and talking up the company? It's not work at all because I love it."

"You were born to it," I said.

He laughed. "You're the one who told me that all along."

"Hold the horses." Dad threw his hands up to pause the conversation. "You all thought that we thought one of you was better than the others?"

Amy and Chris and I all exchanged nods.

"Seems that way," Chris said.

"Well, I've never heard such nonsense," Mom said. "I can't believe that. And I can't believe it led to this fake engagement charade this week. All we've ever wanted was your happiness. Your way. Each of you. You are all blessed with your own talents, and we never expected you to be identical to each other. Your differences make the family better."

That sounded familiar. Josh had been trying to tell me that for years, but only now was I beginning to understand it. I'd spent my whole life thinking I wasn't living up to the examples of my brother and sister, but the truth was we'd all spent our lives pushing each other to be better. In the end, we were our best selves because of each other.

"I'm sorry if we ever made you feel inadequate by praising the accomplishments of your siblings, but I wouldn't take a word of it back," Mom said. "We are proud of each of you. We wanted you all to know that."

"Couldn't have said it better," Dad seconded.

"So, we're okay?" A sense of relief washed through me. I'd imagined they wouldn't want to speak to me again once I'd admitted to lying to them all week. I'd underestimated the ability of family to understand and to forgive.

"You tell us," Mom said.

Chris stepped over and reached for my hand and Amy's. She and I jumped up at the same time and smothered him in a group hug. For the first time in my life, there were absolutely no barriers between us. We leaned into each other with a real confidence that we would always be able to lean on each other when we needed it most.

"We're okay," I said when we finally released each other and stepped back.

Dad shook his head. "Well, if anyone asked me, I'd say you're all a little foolish."

"Well, you raised us," Amy said, wiping at the happy tears forming at the corner of her eyes. "So whose fault is that?"

"Oh, your mother's definitely." He leaned over and planted a kiss on her cheek.

She pushed him away playfully. "I only take credit for the good parts. Anything foolish and I lay full blame on your grandparents. They spoiled you rotten."

"That's what grandparents do," Chris said. He nodded toward Amy. "You'll get your chance."

Mom's eyes sparkled at the thought of that.

Dad clapped his hands together. "If we're all settled then, and no one else has any revelations for the day, how about we get to celebrating Christmas?"

"A fine idea," Mom said. She turned to me. "We would love for Josh to join us."

That erased my budding hope that everything was going to be okay. Josh may not want to join us, for anything, ever again.

~ 24 ~

A Cup of Christmas Cheer

Back in my room, I freshened up and fretted over what to say to Josh. As we'd left Mom's cabin, she told us to take our time and make our way to the atrium this afternoon when we were ready for the family Christmas celebration. I wasn't sure I could be ready today, not if it required confronting my mixed-up feelings for Josh. I needed a solid plan for what to say to him, and I was at a total loss. He was the one I turned to for things like this.

If my brother and sister had admired me my entire life without me ever having a clue about it, could Josh and I have fallen in love this week without meaning to? It was possible. And it was scary. And maybe wonderful?

All the conflicting thoughts bounced around my head as I splashed water on my face and revived my limp hair with a few twists over a curling iron. It gave my hands something to do while I argued with myself in the mirror, and there was no reason I shouldn't look my best for whatever conversation I was going to have with Josh today.

A knock on the hallway door made me jump. I crept toward the peephole, holding my breath. What if it was Josh? Could I pretend I wasn't there? I wasn't ready to talk to him yet.

When I saw Chris standing there, I exhaled my unease and swung the door open.

He'd donned an ugly Christmas sweater with a giant cheerful penguin on the front. "Come on, let me buy you a Christmas cocktail."

"You're not mad at me?"

"I'm not happy that you lied to me all week and made Josh lie to me all week, but I can't let my little sister sit in her room and cry on Christmas. Let's go."

I grabbed my keycard and followed him down the hallway. When he headed down the stairs toward the Atrium Bar, I protested that I wasn't ready to hang out with the rest of the family yet.

"Don't worry," Chris said. "They anticipated your emotional crisis with Josh would take a few hours. They're all on the top deck soaking in some Christmas rays."

"Am I that transparent?"

"The panic on your face was pretty clear when Mom told you to invite him to join us."

If I'd been that easy to read earlier in the week, maybe we could have avoided this mess altogether. I'd expected them to immediately see through my

Josh engagement story. It'd been startling when they hadn't. And that's when it had all started to go wrong.

"I told them you guys needed a little time to work some things out."

"Thanks, Chris."

"You can put it on my good karma tab."

"After this morning, I'm thinking that's getting pretty full."

"No doubt."

As we entered the sun-drenched atrium, the Christmas cheer overwhelmed my senses. They'd added more glistening ornaments to the giant tree and more twinkling lights to all of the small trees around the room. Christmas carols floated softly from the pianist in the corner, and everyone we passed, passengers and staff alike, wished us a Merry Christmas.

That remained to be seen. Being open with my family had surprisingly brought us closer, but I had no idea what being honest with Josh would even look like, let alone what the outcome would be. This could turn out to be the un-merriest Christmas ever.

Chris and I took two stools at the end of the bar, and a bartender in a fluffy Santa hat greeted us with a jolly "Merry Christmas." He poured us the drink of the day, a Cup of Christmas Cheer.

"To family." I raised my glass to the one thing I was thankful for today.

"To a memorable Christmas," Chris toasted.

I'd made it unforgettable for sure. This might be the Christmas I regretted forever. I sipped my drink. The Cup of Christmas Cheer tasted like a delicious White Russian topped with whipped cream and a cherry, but it would take a lot more than that to make this day cheery.

"I'm sorry I lied to you," I said.

Chris frowned. "I'm sorry you felt like you had to. The other day at the Sundeck Bar, it was just me and you. That was your chance to trust me with the truth, you know."

I twirled the cocktail straw around the whipped cream in my drink and tried to spear the cherry. "I know. I was too ashamed. I wanted to tell you. I really did. I tried to tell you, but I couldn't get the words to come out."

"When you said he might not be the one." Understanding crossed his face as he put the pieces of the week together in the new light I'd shed on them this morning.

"Yeah."

"That wasn't quite the same as telling me it was all fake. I had to hear it from Josh last night."

Another thing to add to the list of things Josh had done for me this week. "I didn't mean for that to fall on him to tell you. I handled it all wrong. I should have told you from the beginning."

Chris nodded like that was the most obvious thing in the world. "Yep. You should have."

"Will you forgive me?" I asked.

"If you promise to never do that again."

"Cross my heart." I drew an exaggerated X in the air over my heart.

He handed me the cherry from his drink. "Then you're forgiven."

I took the peace offering. Then I threw my arms around his neck and squeezed. "You're the best big brother."

"Now don't get carried away. That's what got you into trouble in the first place."

"Noted." I settled back on my stool.

"But you can still think I'm awesome. I mean, that part's true." His usual charismatic grin spread across his face. "As long as you realize you are awesome too."

I teased him for being cheesy, but then we lifted our cups to Greyson family awesomeness. At least things were back to normal with Chris. That went a long way toward settling my anxiety over this whole week, knowing I hadn't ruined my relationship with my brother. But I still needed to get back to normal with Josh. He should be here with us like he'd been at the beginning of the week.

"How is he?" I asked.

"He's as big a mess as you are."

That wounded me. "I never meant to hurt him."

"Well, you did a fine job of it. He's moping around the room like he lost his best friend. It took me forever to talk him in off the balcony last night, and it took some serious coaxing to convince him to stay put today until I had time to talk to you."

I chewed on my lip. I still didn't know what I'd say to him today. "I could use some brotherly advice here, Chris. He told me that he loved me for real last night, and I responded by basically telling him he was delusional. I don't think there's any coming back from that."

Chris snorted out a laugh. "That is a pretty rough start, but trust me, Josh loves you despite your full-on denial of it."

"If he does, then he is way too good for me."

Chris nudged my shoulder with his. "You deserve to be loved by a guy like Josh."

I shook my head and tried to shush him, but Chris wouldn't have it.

"Hear me out on this. From the big brother perspective, that guy has done nothing but pretty much worship you since you guys met in high school, and you've done the same for him. So you were both too dumb to see it for over a decade. No time like the present to fix it. I can tell you without a doubt after rooming with him for the week that no one could love you more than he does."

He made the love that I'd convinced myself was fake this week sound so real. What did Chris see that I hadn't ever seen? "How could you know that?"

"I'm not blind, even if you guys are. I've seen you together all week. You are happy, and I mean deliriously happy with him, and he's the same with you. You know what he talks about nonstop when you're not around? You. You know the last thing he thinks about before he sleeps? You. You know the first thing he thinks about in the morning? You. I can't count the number of times I've heard, 'I hope Kate had a great time today.' 'Do you think Kate would like this?' 'I wonder if Kate is up yet.' 'I should get Kate some coffee.' All I've heard is 'Kate... Kate... Kate.' That's been the theme of his week, and if I had to guess, it's been the theme of his life. Josh is undeniably devoted to you."

I tried one more time to dismiss that. "He was supposed to be putting on a show. We were supposed to be engaged, remember? It was all an act."

Chris nodded and took a long draw on his Cup of Cheer. "Yeah, yeah. I get that. But I can tell you that Josh stopped acting about the time we went dancing on the beach in St. Maarten."

"What makes you say that?"

"Because a guy doesn't hold a friend in his arms the way he held you that night."

I wanted to protest that he'd read the situation wrong, but I had to admit that something had shifted between Josh and me that night. After our near-miss kiss, he had clung to me as much as I'd clung to him. That's what Chris had seen. That's when I'd gotten all turned around about my feelings for Josh. Was that when he started to fall in love with me?

Since then, Josh had hardly mentioned our fake engagement. He'd glossed over it or dismissed it when I brought it up. He'd told me to stop thinking about breaking up and just enjoy the week with him. He'd been sweet enough to shop for my entire family for Christmas and take me for a wintry Christmas afternoon of ice skating. He'd done small, silly things like make me a heart-shaped cookie and big, time-consuming things like learn new dance moves for the ball. He'd spent last night getting soaked on my balcony trying to get me to talk to him after our argument. Josh had always been a great friend, but everything he'd done this week was above and beyond friendship. That was Josh in love. I'd seen it before. He went all out for the girls he dated. But this week, he'd done it all for me. Josh was in love with me.

I stared, dumbfounded, at my reflection in the mirror behind the bar. Was I in love with him, too?

"And," Chris added, "he showed me what he bought you for Christmas. That is definitely not a present for someone who is just a friend."

"What?" I whipped my attention back to him. "You can't tease like that. What did he get me?"

"Oh, I am not telling. That is between you two, but I can tell you without a doubt, that guy is head over heels in love with you, Katie."

Whatever the gift was, it was too much. "I told him not to buy me anything. Coming along on the trip was supposed to be his present to me."

"Yeah, well, that ship has sailed." Chris chuckled at his own pun.

I blew out a long breath. "Now what do I do?"

Chris turned to face me. "First, you figure out if you really love him. You owe him the truth. Then when you come to your senses and realize that you are in love with him, you do something amazing to show him exactly how much you love him. Because right now, he's as heartbroken as heartbroken gets. And he's sulking around my room, so I'm not going to get any peace until you guys make up."

My heart ached as I struggled through the possibilities in my head. I asked the question that had been holding me back, the one that scared me the most. "What if it doesn't work out? I could lose my best friend."

"You can't live your life afraid of what might happen. I believe you're the one who told me that."

"Why do you have to remember all my quotable advice? Do you know how irritating that is?"

He patted my shoulder. "All part of being the best big brother ever."

"I don't believe I said 'ever.'"

He laughed and ordered us two more Cups of Christmas Cheer.

I fidgeted with my cocktail napkin as Chris hummed along to the Christmas carols and struck up a conversation with the bartender. I half-listened and mulled over the brotherly advice.

I owed Josh the truth, and the more I thought about it, the more I knew exactly what that was. Whether we were laughing over souvenirs in St. Maarten or taking one of our sunset strolls in Austin, I loved being with Josh, and I loved who I was with him. I never had to be anything but myself, and it was my best self—the one that only he knew. That kind of intimacy only came with time and devotion. I'd seen it before. I'd admired it for years in my parents' relationship. I couldn't believe it'd taken me this long to see that that was what I had with Josh.

I'd spent my life chasing a fleeting version of romantic love that was all wrong. It really was as simple as turning to the man who had stood by my side for so long and seeing the love that bound us together.

I jumped off the barstool. For the first time this week, I knew exactly what I needed to do. "Will you do me a favor, Chris?"

"Name it," he said.

"Get Josh ready for dinner and back here for our family meetup."

"You got it. What are you going to do?"

Hope that in the next few hours I could make the ideas spinning through my head into reality. "Show Josh that I'm crazy about him."

~ 25 ~

WORTH A THOUSAND WORDS

I PRACTICALLY RAN to the concierge desk. I was a woman on a mission to prove her love, and I needed to do it in spectacular fashion. If the situation were reversed, if I had spilled my heart to Josh and told him I was in love with him and he'd flat-out told me that I was a fool, that the love I professed was impossible, then I would have been absolutely crushed. The thought that I'd done that to Josh nauseated me. I had to do something extraordinary to show him how sorry I was, how wrong I'd been, and how much I loved him.

"Hello, ma'am. What can I assist you with?" the man behind the concierge counter greeted me with the usual chipper Cherish Cruises welcome.

"I need to paint," I said.

"The art gallery is on deck 8."

"No, I don't want to buy a painting. I want to make a painting. Is there somewhere I could do that on this ship?"

"Ma'am, I'm sorry," he explained as if he heard this request every day. "We do not have art supplies onboard."

My heart sank. Painting for Josh would show him exactly what he meant to me, but this guy in his neatly pressed pink and blue uniform was calmly telling me that my brilliant plan was impossible. I couldn't accept that.

"This is life or death important."

That earned me an arched brow.

"Okay, not life or death, but it's a matter of the heart. It's the only way to mend a heart that I'm afraid I broke. And I need to do it today, for Christmas."

He softened at my pleading. "I wish I could help you, ma'am."

"I wish you could, too." My bubble of hope burst. After everything Josh had done for me this week, he deserved more than an apology, and my best idea for showing him how I felt was apparently not an option on short notice on a cruise ship. Dejected at failing so quickly at my grand scheme for redemption, I turned to leave.

I ran headlong into the hostess from the cookie baking event.

"Excuse me," she said as she held her hands out to make sure I didn't tumble over from bumping into her.

"My fault," I said. "Sorry."

I straightened up and stepped back from the immaculate woman. Her expertly pressed blue and pink Cherish uniform hugged her slender curves, and not one hair of her soft dark curls was out of place. Her impeccable appearance reflected the exact opposite of my roiling turmoil. A glimpse of what could be if I ever got it together.

"Did I overhear you asking about painting supplies?" she asked.

Hope crept back into my heart. Did she have a stash of painting supplies? Maybe she had a stash of icing from the cookie baking. I could make that work, a frosting painting. I was willing to try anything to make up with Josh today.

"Yes. I really need to paint today. It's hard to explain."

"But it's a matter of the heart?" she asked.

"I know it sounds crazy, but I have to paint a picture for the guy who could be the love of my life, and I have to do it today."

Her easy laugh said she understood completely. "Sometimes love requires drastic action. I've got some experience with that. Let me see what I can do."

She slipped behind the concierge desk and picked up the phone.

"Merry Christmas," she said into the receiver. "I've got a favor to ask. I have a guest who needs to borrow some painting supplies for a Christmas surprise. Love is hanging in the balance. Could you meet us in the art gallery?"

I held my breath as she listened to the response on the other end of the line.

With a winning smile, she hung up the receiver and said, "Let's get you painting."

I exhaled my relief and almost skipped up the stairs beside her on the way to the art gallery.

She introduced herself as Tori Moore, the ship's event coordinator. When I thanked her profusely for being so understanding and helping me out, she told me the story of how she'd met her boyfriend on a cruise not that long ago and ended up confessing her love for him to the entire ship during the afternoon captain's announcements.

"That's pretty fearless," I said. "And it all worked out?" I wanted any assurance that my plan could actually turn this Christmas from regrettable to remarkable.

"Best day of my life," she said. "I would do it a thousand times over."

She asked what my story was, and I told her the condensed version of the whole sordid tale—from breaking up with Shayne to telling Josh he couldn't be in love with me.

"That is quite the love story," Tori said. "I hope we can help you find the happy ending to it."

I was grateful that she wasn't judging me for my questionable antics this week. She easily could have, and that might have sent me running to my room to hide my embarrassment behind a locked door. A woman as put-together as Tori could have looked down her nose at me, but she seemed to understand that my week had been one long, twisted road to find love, and she found nothing foolish about that. Her confidence in my plan encouraged me that I was finally doing the right thing.

When we reached the art gallery, a familiar-looking, dark-haired guy in a Cherish uniform stood at the entrance with an easel and sketchbook tucked under one arm and a set of brushes and watercolors in his hands.

"Marty," Tori exclaimed and gave him a kiss on each cheek. "This is Kate."

I recognized him as the bartender from the Sundeck Bar as I said hello and thanked him for loaning me his supplies.

"Happy to help a fellow painter," he said in a lighthearted tone that told me it was true.

Tori ushered us into the art gallery and negotiated with the director over where they should set me up. After a couple of minutes of back and forth in forceful, hushed voices, I wasn't sure the director was going to let me paint in her gallery at all. She did not appear to be pleased with the idea, and I heard the words "highly unorthodox" escape her pursed lips. Tori kept her composure throughout the exchange, and ultimately, the director relented and allowed

Marty to set up the easel near the windows at the entrance. This way, I would have good light and not block the view of any of the artwork, but I would also be in full view of any passersby. The thought of an audience was unsettling. I hardly showed anyone my finished work, let alone allowed them to watch me work. But I reminded myself this was all for Josh. He was well worth the stress of a few strangers seeing me paint.

Tori snagged a small display table from the hallway for me to use as a work table for the watercolor pans and brushes. Marty got a couple of water glasses from the nearest bar to dip the brushes in. Then he tore a clean page from his large sketchbook and attached it on the easel with binder clips.

It was beautiful, high-quality paper with deckle edges on three sides, and his paints were pro quality, not the beginner set you'd get at a craft store. I told him I would pay him for the materials, but he wouldn't hear of it.

"When someone needs something, you give it freely," he said.

Words I tried to live by. "I will pass it on. I promise. I can't tell you how much I appreciate this."

"No worries," he said. "I've been in love. You've got to do what you can to hold onto it while it lasts."

Spoken like someone who had loved well, and possibly lost it. I wanted to ask him about it, but I didn't want to pry, especially not in front of the gallery director. It was none of her business.

She quickly lost interest in "the spectacle" and retreated to the back of the gallery. Marty excused himself to get to work at the Sundeck Bar, and Tori hung around long enough to make sure I was settled and had everything I needed. Then she told me to call the concierge desk when I was done, and we'd set up a display for Josh.

I thanked her again and tried not to panic at the word "display." That was the whole point of this—to put my love for Josh on full display—but that didn't lessen my anxiety over exhibiting my work in public. That was something I had never done, and it made my belly flip around like the flying fish we'd seen launching themselves in the waves off our balcony this week.

I couldn't think about that while I painted though. I had to calm myself down and focus. Once they'd left me alone with the paints, that was easier to do. I loved watercolor. I'd been thrilled to see that's what Marty had. I could work in oil or even acrylic, but I found something calming about watercolor. It took patience and planning, but it was also very forgiving of mistakes. Errant brush strokes often ended up mixing beautifully into unintended elements. I stared at the white paper for a good ten minutes before I started, imagining where the brush strokes would fall, which colors I would paint wet to bleed into each other, which spaces to leave untouched to keep the right amount of white space in the work. When I had the full idea in my head, I dipped the first brush into the water and into the deepest blue hue on the pans. Then I let inspiration guide my strokes.

I was fully into the relaxing rhythm of it when the first passengers wandered by.

"I love those colors," one of the women said.

"That's beautiful," said another.

Their compliments warmed me from the inside out. I was creating something beautiful for Josh, and I was no longer afraid of anyone seeing that. He deserved the best that I could give him, so I thought of him as I painted. I thought of everything I loved about him—his giving nature, his good-humored way, his easy laugh. I put all my love for him into every brushstroke.

~ 26 ~

ON DISPLAY

TORI HELPED ME straighten the finished painting on the easel beside the atrium Christmas tree. It had taken me all afternoon to complete, and I could have spent a couple more weeks fussing with it, but overworking a piece can diminish the original vision anyway. This was what I'd had time for—the raw version of it, the truth of my love for Josh. Now on display for the entire cruise ship, it should have made me nervous as passengers walked by and took in the gentle wave of my brush strokes and the variant hues of blue and orange and purple in the ocean and sunset painted there, but tonight I wasn't worried about what they thought. I anxiously waited for Josh to see it. His was the only opinion I cared about, and I second-guessed whether he would really appreciate it, whether it would be enough for him to see what he really meant to me. I paced beside the tree and tried to stay out of people's Christmas photos as they paused in front of it to capture one last vacation memory on their way to dinner.

In half an hour, we were scheduled for the Chef's Supper Dad had booked the family as an engagement celebration for Josh and me. Dad had insisted we go regardless of the engagement being fake because, in his words, "We have a lot to celebrate as a family today. We should take the opportunity while we have it." I wasn't going to feel like celebrating anything if this went sideways with Josh.

And, as if those doubts weren't worry enough, the family was on hand to witness whatever was about to happen. Chris had caught them up on what he knew of my plan this afternoon, so they'd all been waiting with reassuring words for me when I'd first run into the atrium. Once they'd seen the painting and realized the full plan, they'd showered me with compliments on the work and told me what a great idea it was. Now, Mom and Dad and Amy and Jacob all took turns giving me encouraging smiles as they lounged in the wingback chairs by the atrium windows. I wished I could be as relaxed as they looked, dressed in their Christmas best, sipping champagne and sparkling juice, watching the sunset over the sea.

I fidgeted with the aquamarine bracelet Josh had given me. I'd paired it with my red paisley maxi dress for Christmas. I'd barely had time to change, but Tori had graciously offered to transport the painting from the art gallery to the atrium while I ran to my room to slip into my Christmas dress. After helping me set the easel up, she'd withdrawn to a dark corner by the bar to see how the night unfolded. She was talking with Antonio and some passengers, but she gave me a thumbs up when she caught my eye. I wished I had her confidence. I wasn't sure at all that I'd done the right thing here. Maybe I should have gone straight to Josh's room to talk to him instead of getting Chris to bring him to this very public space. If Josh had come to his senses today and decided that I was right last night and we were better off as friends, then I had set myself up for a devastating heartbreak in front of my whole family and half the ship. I had not thought this through. What was I doing?

For probably the hundredth time in the last five minutes, I glanced up the grand staircase that wound down into the atrium, and my breath caught in my throat. Josh and Chris rounded the corner at the top. Josh wore a simple white button-up with a red tie and black slacks, but he'd never looked so good. I was undeniably drawn to him now that I'd let myself hope our love could be real. I wanted to run up those stairs and into his arms, but the fear that he wouldn't welcome that kept my feet firmly planted by the easel. His eyes swept the room and landed on the painting. I couldn't read his reaction, straight-faced and unsmiling, so unlike Josh. His brow furrowed, and for one heart-stopping moment, I worried he would turn on his heel and head right out of my life forever.

But he didn't. He walked slowly down the steps to my side.

"It's beautiful," he said in a measured tone. "That's one of my all-time favorite nights."

"Mine too," I confessed.

The night we'd danced on the beach till almost dawn. I'd wanted to stay in his arms forever. So that's the way I'd painted us—two silhouettes dancing on the sand as the waves lapped at the shore and the stars twinkled through the twilight.

Josh stuffed his hands in his pockets and let an agonizing moment pass before he spoke again. "I want to apologize. I never should have assumed that you felt the same way I did. I didn't mean to overstep. The last thing I wanted was to push you away. I shouldn't have kissed you like that. I got caught up in our charade, and I don't want it to come between us. I wanted to tell you that the moment you left me last night. It's what I should have said on the back of the ship with you. I'm sorry, and I'll do whatever I can to make it up to you. I don't want to ruin our friendship over this."

My heart dropped into my stomach. Was he saying what I'd dreaded he might say? That we should just be friends? Could I let that happen? Could I go back to being his best friend and nothing more? The apology I'd rehearsed in my head all day tumbled out of my mouth. "I'm sorry too. I was afraid that it wasn't real. I didn't want to risk what we've always had on what might not last."

The corner of his lips curled up hopefully. "Then we can work through this?"

I shook my head. No. That was wrong. I didn't want to work through this and come out the same as before. I didn't want to give up on the love I felt for him. I had to tell him that. Now or never. And never wasn't an option. I started talking before I could convince myself not to. "It's too late for that."

His face fell, and I panicked that I was saying this all wrong, but I couldn't stop now.

I rambled on, "I can't go back. I mean, I don't want to go back. I don't want you to want that either. I'm getting this all mixed up, but I'm trying to say that you were right. I was wrong. We can't deny that something happened this week. Something unexpected and unexplainable. We can't dismiss these feelings and pretend they aren't real or that they aren't there. Because they are. They are very real." I licked my lips and sucked in a deep breath. Staring into those deep brown eyes that were searching me for answers, I found the courage to say the thing I'd been too scared to say last night. "I'm in love with you, Josh. I love you."

His face lit up with his broadest grin. "I was hoping you'd say that."

Relief started to wash through me and untie the knot of anxiety that'd been tightening in my chest. "You were?"

He took my hands in his. "You mean everything to me."

Those words sent my heart fluttering wildly. I didn't think anything could make me happier.

"And now I have a question for you."

"Anything," I said.

He lowered down on one knee, and time stopped. I'm pretty sure the earth quit spinning for a minute when he placed a blue heart-shaped diamond ring in my upturned palm. Of all the possible things I thought he might say or do when I told him that I loved him, I hadn't imagined this.

"I found the right girl," he said, "and I'm not hesitating. There's no doubt holding me back. You are the one. You've always been by my side, and I can't imagine facing a day without you. Will you marry me, Katie? I would be honored to call you Wife."

I could hardly breathe, let alone think what to say, so I said the first silly thing that popped into my head, "That's a nickname I'll answer to."

He exhaled a gentle laugh. "So that's a yes?"

In Josh's eyes, I saw everything I'd ever wanted—a man who understood me better than I understood myself sometimes, a man who had always been there for me and always would be, a man who loved me exactly as I was, and a man I loved with all my heart.

"Yes."

He slipped the sparkling ring onto my trembling finger, and it fit perfectly, like it was meant to be there. I wrapped my arms around his neck to hug him close, and he picked me up, spinning me around and laying light kisses all over my cheeks. I found his soft lips with mine and let myself get lost in him for one long, magnificent moment.

When he finally set me down, we were surrounded by congratulatory hugs from my overjoyed family and a host of well-wishers in the atrium. We had our picture taken in front of the giant Christmas tree and soaked in every bit of the merry celebration until it was past time to head for the Chef's Supper. Then Josh took my hand in his and led the way to our real engagement dinner.

Epilogue

THE GENTLE SWAY of the ship rocked me as I lay in bed, but it didn't do any good. I was too excited to sleep. I'd waited more than a year for tomorrow when Dad would walk me down the aisle on the front of the cruise ship at sunset, and I would say "I do" to my best friend and the love of my life. Everything was in place. I had the perfect dress, and the perfect flowers, and the perfect guy. Now I needed a perfect night's sleep to make sure I didn't show up to my own wedding with giant dark circles under my eyes.

I twisted the diamond ring on my finger and opened my eyes. The digital clocked flipped forward to 12:01. It was officially my wedding day. I had to get some sleep. I slung a pillow over my head and tried to calm my thoughts, but instead of the soothing silence I wanted, I heard a soft tap-tap-tap.

Had I imagined that? I pulled the pillow down to hear better.

Tap-tap. Tap-tap.

The sound of fingertips on glass. I smiled. Apparently Josh couldn't sleep either.

I threw the covers back and straightened my oversized sleep shirt that read, "Bride." A gift from Amy and Jacob. They'd given Josh a matching t-shirt that read, "Groom." I wondered if he was wearing it tonight. Probably. Our love was exactly that kind of silly.

I quickly finger-brushed the tangles out of my hair as I reached for the balcony curtain. I slid it back to see Josh smiling in at me. Standing there in his "Groom" t-shirt and plaid pajama pants with his messy hair haloed in the moonlight, he was as casually suave as ever. I couldn't wait to marry him.

I opened the door and stepped out to join him. The rough surface of the deck still held the heat of the day against the soles of my feet, and the night air swirled in pleasant eddies around us as the cruise ship moved through the night.

"Don't you know it's bad luck to see the bride before the wedding?" I asked as I tucked my hair behind my ears to keep it from blowing across my face.

"I don't think it counts if we haven't
still the night before."

I rested my hands on the railing and looked out
into the beautiful night. Without a cloud in the sky,
the moon shone its long, bright reflection
uninterrupted across the dark waters. "We should
both already be asleep. It's going to be a long day
tomorrow."

"You mean a wonderful, unforgettable day,
right?"

I raised a playful brow. "That remains to be
seen."

"Is that a challenge?"

Before I could answer, he slipped over to his side
of the balcony and snatched a present from the table
there. He handed me a flat package wrapped in
shining silver paper with an oversized white bow.

"What's this?"

"I wanted to give you your present before we got
caught up in the festivities."

"You're too sweet." I kissed him on the cheek. I
hadn't thought of exchanging presents before we
started the day. "I don't have yours. I didn't trust
myself to not give it to you too early. Chris has it."

His eyes flicked to his balcony door. "You hid it
in my own room?"

"I figured you wouldn't look there."

"Well, now I will," he said with a hint of
mischief.

"Don't you dare."

Even if he poked around the room, all he'd find was a hand-painted card with a homemade coupon for the "ultimate honeymoon adventure." I was keeping the real gift a surprise until we got to Hawaii. I'd finally gotten him the perfect present, and I wanted to savor the giving of it as long as possible. I'd booked a private guide to take us kayaking down the Napali Coast. Josh was going to love it.

"Fine," he said. "You can keep me in suspense if you want, but I can't wait to give you this. Will you please open it?"

I eyed him curiously as I ran my hands around the present. It was magazine size, but I was pretty sure he hadn't gotten me a magazine for our wedding. I had no idea what it could be. I thought most grooms gave their brides jewelry or something, but leave it to Josh to be inventive. I ripped into the beautiful silver and white package. Under the delicate wrapping was a plain manila envelope. That was more confusing than revealing. I gave him a questioning look. He only smiled wider.

I opened the envelope to find a stack of plain paper inside. I slid it out and read the top.

"Commercial Lease Agreement? I don't understand."

"That antique store next to my coffee shop is moving, so their space came up for lease."

"And you're expanding?" That would be great for his business, but kind of a weird wedding present. Was he asking me to work at his expanded coffee shop? We had been throwing around ideas for what I should do after we were married, whether I should stay at my current yoga studio or look for something else, but we hadn't settled on anything.

He shook his head. "I leased it for you."

"For me?"

"So you can finally open your own yoga studio. Maybe decorate with your artwork. Whatever you want. It's all yours."

I was speechless. I stared at the contract in my hands in disbelief. No one had ever done anything remotely this wonderful for me in my entire life.

"You don't like it?" Concern cracked his voice.

"It's too much."

He laid a warm hand on my cheek and tilted my face up to meet his adoring gaze. "It's an opportunity. That's all. You will make it something amazing."

The way he believed in me made me think that together we would make all our dreams come true. "It's the most perfect thing anyone has ever given me. I couldn't love anything more. I couldn't love you more."

He swept me into his arms then and kissed me with all the passion that half a lifetime of friendship brought to our love.

I Cherish Your Thoughts

Dear Reader,

If you enjoyed *Cherish St. Maarten*, please take a few moments to leave a book review on the Amazon review page for *Cherish St. Maarten*. Book reviews help connect the authors you love with more readers like you.

Spread the love!

Cherish,
Lynette Paul

SNEAK PEEK: HEART OF THE RIVER

Read on for a sneak peek at Book 1 in the Cherish Adventures Sweet Romances Series: *Heart of the River*.

WHEN I PULLED into the gravel parking lot at the put-in point, I saw the "Save the Spotted Turtle" bumper sticker on the raft trailer parked there, and I knew trouble was waiting.

That was Mark Kovack's rig. No doubt about it. He ran the other Snake River rafting expedition company through Hell's Canyon. He shouldn't be at the launch point at the same day and time as me. Especially not today. My clients were too important this week to start off with any kind of conflict with Mark, but there he was with his raft already nosed into the river ready to load.

I parked my van and trailer in the usual spot in the shade of the cottonwoods and turned to my clients in the back. Ryan Anastasi sat with his teenage niece and nephew, waiting for the flawless, five-star, private week on the river I'd promised them. I gave them a smile to hide the anxiety stirring in my chest.

"I'll be just a moment, Mr. Anastasi."

"Please, call me Ryan," he said. Then he narrowed his handsome hazel eyes as though he could sense that something was awry. His keen business instincts were what had convinced me that he might be the perfect buyer for my gourmet guiding business, 5-Star Sandbars. They'd certainly never led him astray in his twenty years of growing tech startups from nothing to millions of dollars in net worth.

"Anything wrong?" he asked.

"I'm sure it's just a misunderstanding." I nodded toward Mark, who was helping his clients out of his van in the shade on the opposite side of the gravel parking lot near the ranger's hut.

"What can I do to help?" Ryan asked. He looked ready to jump in and handle whatever the situation might be.

I didn't need rescuing here. And I didn't need my potential buyer to think that anything could be wrong. "I'll get it cleared up, and we'll get on our way. Wait here, please."

Before he could argue, I grabbed the waterproof bag where I kept my permit and paperwork and hopped out to see what Mark thought he was up to. I had the permit for takeoff this morning, and the

Forest Service controlled river traffic tightly. They wouldn't double issue.

Mark was already unloading his gear. He looked the same as ever, effortlessly comfortable and yet completely confident in his old Jimmy Eat World T-shirt and cargo shorts. His wavy brown hair was always on the verge of needing a haircut, and his deep brown eyes were the kind you could get lost in if you weren't careful. He finally stopped arranging his dry bags once I'd crossed the whole parking lot and stopped right next to him.

He greeted me with his ridiculously charismatic grin. "Carlie Martin, to what do I owe the pleasure?"

I crossed my arms. His charms hadn't worked on me since that summer in college we'd spent guiding together in Costa Rica. That water was miles under the bridge now. "I'm pretty sure you owe it to the fact that you are trying to steal my permit time."

He took a step back from me. "Whoa. That's a pretty big accusation. Why would I poach your permit?"

"That's what I'm asking. I'm standing right here with my clients waiting in the van, but here you are unloading your gear like the river belongs to you."

He threw his hands up in the air like he might be surrendering. "Just hold on a minute."

"Look, I know this is your first summer back in ten years, but you have to follow the rules around here. This isn't Costa Rica or wherever you've been lately." I knew exactly where he'd been—biking tours in Moab, deep sea fishing in Kauai, hiking in Yosemite, fly fishing in Alaska. If there was an adventure tour, he'd taken a turn at guiding it. His father bragged about him every time he got a tattered postcard in the mail. But I wasn't about to tell him I knew that, and I certainly wasn't going to let him come home and sweet-talk his way onto my river during my permitted put-in time.

Mark reached into his back pocket and pulled out a folded piece of paper. "I've got a permit for today, Carlie. Put-in on August 19 at 10:00 a.m."

He handed me the crumpled paper. Only Mark would keep his permit in his back pocket. Mine was, of course, encased safely in a waterproof bag with my detailed itinerary for the week, my backup itinerary, my emergency preparedness plans, and my satellite phone.

I unfolded the paper, and it did appear to be an official National Forest Service permit issued for the exact same day and time as mine.

"This doesn't make any sense." I left Mark with his partially loaded raft, and I stalked toward the ranger hut at the edge of the lot. We would clear this up with Dan. He should be working the hut, as he did every Saturday, to direct wayward tourists toward the hiking trails that wound for miles up the cliffs overlooking the river.

Mark followed me through the front door into the welcoming shade from the summer day. An old Smokey the Bear animatron greeted us from the far side of the room. Topographical maps of the Hells Canyon National Recreation Area and the Wallowa-Whitman National Forest lined the walls. Dan knew every trail detailed there and then some. He leaned back in his chair with his well-worn hiking boots propped up an old steel desk. He held up a solitary old finger that looked, much like Dan himself, like it had been whittled from the basalt walls of the canyon he loved so much. He finished the passage he was reading in his dog-eared copy of Desert Solitaire before he looked up.

"Hey, Carlie. Mark. What can I do you for this fine morning?" Dan asked. His graying mustache waggled gently with every word.

I was confident this would go well. Dan and I had developed a mutual respect for each other over the years. He had a real passion for this place, and he liked my staunch commitment to eco-tourism: Leave no trace. Take only pictures and memories.

"We've got a problem." I handed him the permits.

He read them over and looked up at us with a questioning face. "Looks all in order to me. What's the fuss?"

"The fuss? They're issued for the same day and time with all the same campsites. We're not a joint expedition," I said.

"Looks like you are," Dan said.

"But how can that be? I specifically applied for a private permit," I argued.

Mark jumped in, "The main Park office said today was open."

"Well, it's obviously not," I said.

Dan scratched his unbrushed mop of gray hair. That was a sure sign he was about to say something I wasn't going to like. "Didn't you all attend the new regulations meeting last Tuesday?"

"No, Dan. I'm on the river on Tuesdays," I said.

"Same here," Mark said.

At least we agreed on one thing.

Dan sniffed and leaned forward in his chair. That was as business-like as he ever got. "I don't set the dates. But if you had attended, you would have heard about the new regs going into effect immediately."

"Shouldn't those have been posted?" Mark asked.

"Of course they would be posted," I said. "When you've been running this river for more than a few weeks, you'll learn that new regs get posted right there."

I pointed to the wall between Dan's desk and the front door. My mouth dropped open. There, on a sparkling new white piece of paper taped to the wall, was a freshly printed new regulation notice, effective August 19.

"Well, you're both right," Dan said. "Hung that up this morning. Due to the high permit demand, every river expedition permit must be issued for a minimum of six rafters, plus guides. I'm guessing since you had three, Carlie, and Mark here had three, they just put you together."

"That makes sense," Mark said.

"What?" I ripped the paper off the wall as if reading it any closer would make the news any less worse. "That doesn't make any sense."

Dan shrugged and handed us back our permits. "Well, sense or not, that's how it is. You either go together or you don't go."

MARK WATCHED CARLIE push her way out the door without another word.

Dan gave him a wink and a smile. "Some things are worth chasing," he said as he propped his boots back on the desk and picked up his book.

Mark sighed and caught the screen door before it slammed shut behind her. He followed her out into the heat of the day. Carlie Martin got under Mark's skin the way no woman ever had. She had the uncanny ability to be better at everything than anyone else. Except for relaxing. She almost always failed miserably at that. The only time he'd seen her truly relax was that summer they guided together on the Pacuare River in Costa Rica. At the end of a long week on the river, they would take a six-pack of Ortega to the beach and lay under the stars, listening to the ocean lap at the shore.

The carefree girl she had been then is what he saw when he looked at her now, hidden somewhere inside her all-business exterior.

About halfway back to his van, she stopped under the glaring sun and whirled on him.

"Look, if we're in this together, we need some ground rules for the week."

"I wouldn't expect any less from you," he said.

"Good. I'm glad we understand each other. I've been guiding this river for a decade. You follow my lead and stay out of my way, and we'll make it through this week."

"I have done this before," Mark interjected.

"My clients..." Carlie paused and took a long look at the van. Then she squinted at the river.

They may have spent the last ten years apart, but Mark knew Carlie better than she probably wanted to admit. He knew her tells. She was the kind of person that always looked you in the eye and told you exactly what she was thinking. If she was avoiding his gaze, she was hiding something. And now he wanted to know exactly what she felt like she needed to hide about her clients. The fact that there was something she wasn't willing to say about them made him all the more curious and determined to find out.

She continued, "My clients paid handsomely for a private, luxury tour of Hell's Canyon. I expect to provide that."

"I see," Mark said. That wasn't so unusual. It certainly shouldn't give Carlie any pause. Mark wondered if it was his presence flustering her this morning. They hadn't really talked since he'd been back, and he knew they should. They hadn't parted on the best terms ten years ago. There were so many things he'd wanted to say over the years, but it wasn't a conversation for a cross-country phone call. The fact that he and his father communicated better through postcards than in person meant that he'd never really made it back to Hell's Canyon. Until now.

"I also expect you to keep those teenagers under control this week." She nodded toward Mark's clients, who were all looking miserable in their own ways.

Kristie Reynolds stood in the middle of the parking lot in her strappy sandals and freshly pressed khaki shorts and spoke insistently into her cell phone. Kristie's jaw had dropped in shock when Mark explained that there would be absolutely no cell coverage once they launched into the canyon. As an executive concierge, she apparently had crucial work that could not be neglected for five days on the river and needed to give detailed instructions to her assistant before they shoved off. She reminded Mark of Carlie in that way. A little bit of a control freak.

But Kristie was a control freak he was determined to please this week. She was here to scout the trip for executive retreats. She could throw him enough business to bring his father's guiding service back into the black. All Mark had managed to do after his dad had taken ill was run the business even further into the red. He'd been failing his father his whole life. This was his one last chance to prove himself to the man who'd taught him everything.

Mark hadn't expected that part of the challenge for the week would be Kristie's two teenage sons. "If you can handle my kids, you can handle the execs," she'd said.

Once he'd met the family, Mark suspected there was an ulterior motive for the trip with her kids. They obviously weren't connecting on any level, not that he could judge them for that given his own relationship with his father, but he wanted to make it better. He always wanted to make it better, even if he didn't know how.

Kristie's sixteen-year-old, Joe, was trying to skip rocks across the gentle flow of the river. Kristie paused long enough in instructing her assistant to yell at him to get back from the water's edge. Mark guessed those kids had never been far off the leash and was willing to bet that leash had gotten noose-like whenever their father had disappeared from the picture. The twelve-year-old, Adam, had obviously given up on tugging on it. He was still in the van reading his iPad—the only thing Mark had seen him do since he picked them up that morning.

Mark had seen five days on a river transform a lot of people. He hoped to make this trip what this family needed and, as a bonus, land the new bookings he desperately needed. What he certainly didn't need was Carlie's anal-retentive inability to relax keeping Kristie on edge.

"Well?" Carlie asked.

Mark realized he must have missed her last instructions. "Well what?"

Carlie put her hands on her hips. Even at her most demanding, she was still beautiful. Her long hair was neatly tied up into a bun with a couple of thin wisps escaping control around her face. She made quick-drying shorts and a tank top look like they belonged on a runway.

"Do you think you can handle that?" she said.

If there was one thing Mark knew, it was that once he was on the river, he could handle anything. He didn't hesitate to agree. "Yeah, I can handle that."

If you enjoyed this sneak peek of *Heart of the River*, follow Lynette Paul on Amazon and sign up for Lynette Paul's newsletter at LynettePaul.com to receive notifications about this and future publications.

ABOUT LYNETTE PAUL

Lynette Paul lives in the hills of the Ozarks and loves traveling to new places where there's always inspiration waiting for the next sweet romance in the Cherish series.

You can follow Lynette's latest adventures on Facebook (@lynettepaulwrites) and Instagram (@cherishadventures). And you can sign up for the Cherish newsletter at LynettePaul.com to receive updates about new releases and works in progress!

Made in the USA
Las Vegas, NV
27 December 2023